LOVE IN THE HIGHLANDS

COMPLETE

FIONA KNIGHTLEY

Copyright © 2023 by Fiona Knightley

All rights reserved.

No part of this book may be reproduced in any form or by any electronic or mechanical means, including information storage and retrieval systems, without written permission from the author, except for the use of brief quotations in a book review.

HIGHLANDER'S PROPOSAL

LOVE IN THE HIGHLANDS

FIONA KNIGHTLEY

HIGHLANDER'S PROPOSAL

*R*ain pattered against the tall widows of Darra's room as she sat with her knees curled to her chest, watching the heavy gray clouds dim the world beyond. She wiped her eyes with the sleeve of her dress, staining the delicate fabric with salty tears. Typically, her eyes were as green as the rolling hills surrounding the keep, but recently they've been dull and clouded with red flushed skin surrounding them. She would be marrying Laird Samuel Carrigan, and she had no choice in the matter.

It was not unusual for women of her stature to be married in arrangements like these. Her mother's wedding to her father, Laird Guthrie Sloane, had been arranged to end a land dispute. In the end, they found comfort with each other and had four children. Darra could only hope her union would be as fruitful, but she was about to marry Laird Samuel 'The Cruel.' He was known throughout the Sloane clan as a monster in battle, tales of his brutish nature travelled quickly throughout their lands, and Darra had overheard too many stories to feel comfortable in the arrangement.

She wished Callum could take her away. Each time she thought of him, she felt her heart sink within her, and she felt the urge to sob. Darra loved him so much it hurt, and the thought of lying with another man killed her - a man who had slain her people with a cruel smile, no less. She tried not to let the thoughts of his cruelty overtake her mind but failed. She imagined he would be ruthless to her, ravage and force himself on her. He would imprison her in his keep to use when he wanted, perhaps even kill her. They were to wed, bringing an end to the war between their clans, but what if it was a ploy of his to kidnap Darra and force her father to give up lands?

I need to speak to my father soon, Darra thought as she stood up from her daybed and rushed to the mirror. She brushed her fingers through her fiery red hair separating curls with each stroke. She wore a green satin gown with long flowing sleeves and a skirt. Her bodice was decorated with golden filigree. Others had always told her she was pretty, and she had grown fond of her curves - soft and slender with supple rosy skin - Darra was beginning to feel like she had come into herself, but now all the authority she had was being taken. She was losing the decision to choose her lover, and she felt as though her own body would not belong to her much longer.

The Sloane keep was full of life. Even amid a war, it was a bright escape from the darkness surrounding the clan. All folk knew that if they needed anything, they were welcome to seek it out at the keep. While the Sloane family was considered noble to the rest of the clan, they never saw themselves that way. The clan was their family.

~

Laird Samuel Carrigan's tired eyes ran over the thin scribbles of Laird Sloane's letter for the hundredth time. An end to the war. An end. Samuel had dreamed of the war coming to an end his entire life. Since he was a boy of eight when he was given a sword and forced to train, he'd dreamt of the end. But what would his clan think? Would they think him a coward, taking the easy way out, too afraid to continue the fight? *Do they think I'm weak?* So he thought, nearly every morning. Before his father passed, he fought alongside the clan's men in numerous battles. As a result, he earned the title "Samuel the Cruel" for his ruthless conviction on the battlefield and his brute strength. He was respected as a warrior in the clan - feared even - but he worried he had been losing the clan's respect.

This marriage was a means to an end. Samuel was sure the woman he'd marry could never love him. He was taking her away from her home and her people and her choice of a husband. What if she had a lover and he was separating them? He buried the hurt he felt deep within him. He could not show weakness, not now. He had to be strong and show the clan this was the right move. But the part of him, the child who had never been allowed to flourish before he was trained to be a monster, hoped he could be happy in the arrangement. And he hoped Darra Sloane, his new bride-to-be, could find comfort and possibly love with him.

Darra barged through the door to her father's study without a knock. He sat at a large wooden table with his head buried in ledgers and documents he needed to sign. He looked up at her with an annoyed grimace across his thin lips.

"Have ye thought that perhaps this could be a ploy of his?" She started saying as she paced in front of the table anxiously. Her father leaned back and watched her pace with weary eyes. "He could have suggested this to *kill* me! This could be an act of war, father." She slammed her hands dramatically on the opposite end of the table. Laird Guthrie slowly rubbed his fingers against his temples as he watched her.

"Are ye finished?" He replied. Darra crossed her arms and slunk down in a chair across from him. "ye'r marrying Laird Carrigan, and that's final." The annoyance left his small eyes when he saw the disappointment on Darra's face. He reached his hand across the table and held hers. "It's the only way to bring peace. It's for the clan."

"I ken" she whispered, "I'm just afraid." Her father squeezed her hand tighter and took a deep breath.

"If he harms ye in any way, he will live to regret it," he said calmly. Darra knew he meant it. Her father wasn't a fighter and didn't care for the war, but he could be brutal if needed.

Darra brushed her fingers against the stone walls of the keep as she walked back to her chamber to finish packing. She'd miss every detail about these walls; how the exemplary tapestries each told a story, the bright flowers in colourful vases, even the uneven step she always tripped over when she was in a hurry. All of these, and much more, made up her home - her life. And she was leaving it all behind.

She found her sister, Deidre, sitting on her bed when she opened the door. Deidre was only fifteen, but she had a sharp mind. When Darra walked in, Deidre was looking at the floor and tying her hair into a braid. She rested her hands in her lap and looked at her for a moment before speaking.

"ye'r leaving tomorrow?" She asked in her soft voice. Darra nodded her head and walked over to sit next to her. She took her hands in her own and held them tightly.

"Donnae ye worry about me now, I can take care of myself well enough," Darra reassured her. Deidre's small frame shook gently, and Darra held her tightly while she cried.

"What am I supposed to do without ye?" She leaned back and wiped her tears on her sleeve. "First mother and now ye. I'm gonnae be so alone here." Darra tenderly brushed the hair out of her sister's eyes.

"We'll still see each other. And we can always write," Darra said, hoping it would calm her. Deidre nodded her head and took a deep breath to compose herself. "Ye'll do just fine here, without me."

Deidre stayed and helped Darra pack her clothes. They told stories about their childhood and talked fondly of their mother while they decided what clothes and jewelry were worth taking. *What would mother think of this?* Darra thought when they broached the subject. She was a romantic woman, her mother. She'd always told them about how she met their father and how deeply she loved him. Darra always dreamt she would love her husband as much as her mother loved hers. The more she thought of it, the more she felt cheated of her very own happiness.

She hugged her sister tightly as they said goodnight to each other. She felt for her; their mother passed away, leaving them to raise themselves. Thankfully they had help from the servants, but it wasn't the same as a mother's love. Their father had been too busy with the war efforts to be involved in their life. Darra hoped that even though she was leaving, her father would now be able to spend time with Deidre. With the war over, there would be nothing to hold him back. She prayed her sister could have a close relationship with her father, one that Darra had never had.

Samuel rode to the heart of the village in the early evening. He'd sent his advisor and right-hand man to inform the town so they could gather for his announcement. He'd spent all day thinking of the best way to tell the people, but he knew they would think less of him any way he did — that he was taking the easy way out. The Carrigan clan had always been strong and proud - they'd rather die fighting than accept defeat or give up. Samuel had been raised that way as well, but he was tired of it. He hated letting them down, but this is what the clan *needed*.

He slowed his horse as he approached the center of town. The town turned to watch him as he handed his horse to a young boy who worked in the stables. He nodded at the child and patted his shoulders as a thank ye. His stomach knotted and begged him to return to the keep, but he persisted. Silent eyes followed him to the small dais erected in the town square. Typically, the town would gather for announcements related to the war - new battles, recruitment, death announcements - or to watch a public punishment. Samuel had gathered the townsfolk for those reasons more times than he could count, yet this announcement made him nervous, which they never did. *Why?* He asked himself as he tried to steady his hands so no one could see him shaking. The slightest hint of weakness risked losing their respect.

Angus, his advisor, squeezed his shoulder as he approached the stairs to the dais. They nodded, and Samuel ascended the stairs to begin what would undoubtedly be a tumultuous affair.

"Good evening, everyone," Samuel started as he watched the ravaged faces of his folk nod back at him, "thank ye all for coming out today. I've got an important announcement, and I know some of ye will be unhappy. I wanted to take this opportunity to address any concerns myself before the rumours spread." The town murmured to themselves for a moment, and Samuel paused until they stopped. "The war with the Sloane clan will soon be coming to an end." The crowd gasped and looked at each other with excitement and confusion. Samuel scanned the crowd and found a few disgruntled faces; he was sure when they learned why they would be even more so. "All I've ken my entire life is war. I was eight years old and training to slay the people of the Sloane clan in the barracks. And I did just that. I fought alongside our dead brothers, who gave their lives for the clan. Valiant men who left behind wives and children. Children who, if nothing is to change, will someday meet the same end as their fathers. This war has gone on for twenty years. It has stripped our homes of life. I ask ye, when was the last time ye knew peace or joy?" He paused, and the crowd slowly murmured to themselves. Some folk nodded agreeingly, but many grew angry with every word. "I was just a boy, four or five years old, and my mother planned a celebration for my birthday. A few friends came, and we played games and ate sweet cake. All of those friends have since died in battle." The crowd stared at him in silence for a moment. Finally, he calmed himself before delivering the real news. "I will soon be wed to the eldest daughter of Laird Guthrie Sloane. Our union will end the war, and our heir shall unite the clans for future generations to finally know peace."

The crowd clamoured to themselves, occasionally looking back at Samuel in disbelief. The angry men in the clan stormed off after hearing the news. *I'll have to find a way to prove to them this is the right decision.* So he thought to himself as he walked off the dais. Angus grabbed his shoulder and squeezed it with a reassuring smile.

"It's the best option; they'll come to understand it eventually," he said to Samuel as they walked to the stables to get their horses. Samuel only responded with a nod.

~

*D*arra stared at the ceiling in her room, defeated and unable to sleep. She could think of no way to stop the union between her and Cruel Laird Carrigan. She wanted to stay in her clan and marry Callum. She looked towards her door as she heard footsteps approaching. They stopped just before her door and then retreated. A moment later, they came again and stopped. *Who could that be?* She thought as she stood and walked towards the door. She opened it to find Callum standing on the other side as if she'd summoned him with her thoughts. He froze and stared at her. His mouth hung open as if he were trying to say something, but no words came.

She reached for his hand and pulled him into her room. She saw him blush and looked behind him to check for witnesses. Darra laughed at him.

"What if someone sees us?" He said to her in a hushed tone. She just laughed again and embraced him.

"I'll miss ye, Callum," she whispered to him. He held her in his arms for a moment and pulled her away when he realized she was softly crying. He looked her in the eyes and held her face in his hands.

"We've still got a few hours, I can whisk ye away to a faraway land, and we can be together." He wiped tears from her eyes and smiled at her. Darra just shook her head no.

"As much as I'd love that, I cannae," she paused for a few moments and stared into his bright blue eyes. She always thought they resembled gems, so clear and bright, and when the light hit them, it revealed a whole new world within - swirls of green with gold flecks that looked like a cosmic flurry of stars. "I just wish it could have been ye," she whispered. He held her in his arms again and kissed her forehead.

"I know," he said quietly, "I'd give anything to be with ye, Darra." She pulled her head away and quickly leaned in to kiss him. Her lips met his, and she felt an explosion of desire in her chest. He grabbed her face and kissed her for a few moments, then pulled his face away.

"What is it?" She asked him, the hurt she felt reflected in her face.

"This is wrong," he started to say, "It *feels* so right, Darra, but ye'r promised to someone else. We cannae continue this." Darra nodded her head and looked down at her hands.

"Ye'r right. Ye should go," she said to him. Her eyes stung, and she knew she'd soon be crying and didn't want him to see it. Darra stormed to the door and opened it, quickly looking outside to check for any witnesses. Callum walked through the door and turned to look at her one last time, but she closed the door in his face. She stood in front of it, waiting to hear his footsteps fade. When she did, she fell to her knees in front of the door and sobbed.

"Why couldnae it be ye?" She pleaded. After a while, she lay down in bed and fell asleep, soon awakened as her chambermaid began bringing her belongings outside for her to leave for the Carrigan Keep.

The Carrigan Keep was full of people preparing for the wedding. Samuel found it nearly impossible to find a quiet place to think in the days leading up to Darra Sloane's arrival. Servants constantly searched for him to get his opinions on decorations, food, guests, etc. He wanted nothing to do with the planning but found himself forced into it. The day had finally come, and he was to put on the face of a happy bridegroom, but he couldn't muster the ability to lie.

He was standing on his private balcony in his wedding attire, a delicate gold silk tunic with tapered trousers made custom for him by the local tailor. His balcony was one of the few places he could escape for peace. It overlooked the entrance to the keep, and he could see all the comings and goings for miles. Below him were the lush green landscapes and floral patches in the gardens. He saw the horses of the Sloane clan coming; four guards rode in front of a woman he assumed was his bride-to-be. *She's stunning.* He thought to himself as he watched her approach. She was too far away to see in great detail, but he could tell she had vibrant red hair, pale skin, and a slender frame - but most of all, he noticed a curiosity in her as she approached. He could tell she was someone who wanted to learn all she could about the clan, the history, where every path across those rolling green hills led. He could see a hunger for adventure within her. As she approached the keep, Samuel couldn't take his eyes off her.

~

The journey to the Carrigan Keep had been easier than she thought. Part of her hoped there would be a group of bandits or a pack of hungry wolves that would force them to turn around. But that was the stuff of books, and she wasn't as lucky as those women. Callum was supposed to accompany her with the other guards, but this morning he was ill, so another took his place. *Probably for the best.* She thought to herself every time she looked between the other guards. They had nothing to say to her - her father probably warned them against speaking to her. He had always been cautious with the men allowed in her presence - save the one he arranged her to marry.

Darra could not deny the lands in the Carrigan clan were beautiful. She watched clouds float above her and reveal the bright sun as it shone on the moist earth, willing flowers to bloom. The lands were expansive, the hills were bright green and seemingly endless compared to those of her own home, and there were woods here. She had always wanted to explore the woods and see the creatures within them - her own clan's lands had small woodland patches but none as vast as the ones here.

The keep appeared to be quite grand, too. The Sloane Keep was simple and practical; she'd grown up with hardly any decorations or ornaments around her home. Her father felt it was a crude display of wealth and hated the idea of showing off when other people in the clan were desperate for money. The Carrigans didn't seem to care much about that. She rode her horse past beautifully landscaped gardens and inhaled the scent of dew and fresh flowers. The keep itself was a large stone structure, and she could see tall oval-shaped windows and small balconies in front of some of them.

She felt his stare before she even noticed him. A man leaning against one of the balconies was staring at her. She looked at him for a moment and could just make out a cold face and dark hair on a tall, muscular build. The man stood straight, and she saw he was wearing a handsome tunic and trousers. *Could that be him?* Her stomach knotted at the thought of it. Had she just seen her soon-to-be husband? He was intimidating for sure. Her mouth went dry as she neared the entrance of the keep. She looked for the man in the gold tunic but didn't see him. *Surely if that were my betrothed, he'd welcome me to my new home.*

One of the guards accompanying her helped her off her horse and carried her belongings to the entrance. There, waiting for them, were three people; in the middle, an older man with white hair and sagging skin, and on either side were two yeng women who appeared to be chambermaids. The women were identical twins with kind faces and pale orange hair. They seemed to be about Darra's age, if not yenger.

Darra approached the front steps of the entrance with a smile, she was terrified and didn't fully trust these people, but she would be remiss not to give them a chance at first. The older man bowed his head and held his hand out for her. Darra placed her hand in his, and the man softly kissed the back of it. *Surely this isn't him?* She thought nervously, looking at his sallow skin. He was handsome, but the age difference would be nearly impossible to move past for her.

"Darra Sloane, welcome to the Carrigan Clan. I hope ye find the keep to ye'r liking," the older man said with a genuine smile. She smiled and thanked him. "My name is Angus. I work closely with Laird Carrigan, so if ye need anything, please do not hesitate to ask!" She just nodded in response with a smile. She realized she was extremely overwhelmed with this all of a sudden. She thought she had prepared well enough on the trek here, but the actuality set in, and she felt a sense of defeat.

Angus led her inside the keep, and she was taken aback by its beauty. She expected the worst before she arrived. She anticipated dark halls full of cobwebs and macabre decorations - she expected the keep to be a prison to her. But instead, it was vibrant. Eyes fell on her, and people whispered to each other as they rushed through the halls.

"Donnae mind them, normally we'd have a more formal introduction, but they're busy preparing for the wedding tonight," Angus said as he led her up a set of stairs.

"It's tonight?" She asked as she hurried to keep pace and walk next to him on the broad steps.

"Aye, we thought it best to have the ceremony immediately," he replied without further elaboration.

"I'm sorry," Darra said. She fumbled with words in her head for a moment, "I thought I'd have time to meet my betrothed before our union? This all seems rushed. I donnae have any family here; the guards left at the entrance-"

"I'm sorry, m'lady, but this was the compromise to end the hostilities."

Compromise. Is that all I am to these people? So she thought as she followed Angus down a wide hallway. They walked past numerous paintings she could only get quick glimpses of before they stopped in front of a door.

"This is ye'r chamber, m'lady. Kailee and Keiren are ye'r chambermaids, and they will help ye with anything ye need. Now, the ceremony will take place just before sunset, so please be in the chapel then." Angus gave a slight bow and walked back down the hall.

Darra turned the knob and opened her door to find a spacious room with high ceilings and large windows letting in an abundance of daylight. She was again surprised by the warmth of the room. The wind blew past the gauzy fabric curtains and wafted the scent of the fresh cut flowers in the vases to her nostrils. She inhaled and found herself calming just a bit as she thought this might not be as bad a place as she imagined; she'd always allowed her imagination to run wild.

The two chambermaids walked to the large four-poster bed and lifted an elegant white gown for her to see.

"This will look lovely on ye!" The one with a long braid said to her, not sure which twin was which yet. "Laird Carrigan made sure to get ye'r measurements in his letters so it would fit."

"Aye, and the gold ribbons will make ye'r eyes look wonderful!" The other maid said she wore her hair in a loose ponytail. "I'll draw ye a bath so we can start dressing ye."

"Thank ye both," Darra started to say as she walked to the one holding the dress, "might I ask which of ye is Keiren and which is Kailee?" They explained that Keiren was holding the dress with the braid, and Kailee had the ponytail.

After some time, Darra's bath was ready, and she freshened herself up after her trip here. When she was through, the twins began grooming her, combing her hair and tying an elegant braid with tiny gold and green flower petals weaved throughout. Next, they helped her put her dress on and tied it to accentuate her slim waist. When finished, they finally let Darra see herself, and she was astounded at her reflection. She certainly looked the part of a beautiful bride.

~

The few guests Samuel had invited arrived just before sunset. They were led to the chapel and seated to await the ceremony. Samuel stood by the entrance, greeted them with a smile, and thanked them all for coming. He was more nervous than expected; the wedding was not one of love and passion, but this was a critical union nonetheless. *And after seeing my bride riding in...* He caught himself before any other thoughts about her crossed his mind. It wasn't fair to think of her that way right now. She was not here by her own choice, and the last thing he wanted was for her to feel uncomfortable around him because he was lusting after her.

They would need an heir and have to consummate their union at some point to produce one, but he wouldn't force her before she was ready. Most surely, it would take some time for her to get used to him, but he hoped that she might someday learn to love him.

The minister rang a small bell, and all of the guests stood and turned to the door. Samuel cleared his throat and straightened his tunic before walking down the aisle to stand underneath a wooden archway decorated with flowers and a fresh wreath. Standing beside the arch was his stepmother, Shannon, who even now wore a scowl on her thin pale face. Next to her was Samuel's brother, Duncan. He was not yet ten and eager for the ceremony to end so he could play. He reached the end of the aisle and turned to face the doorway as the minister rang the bell again.

He gulped when he saw her. She was more beautiful than he thought. He'd only seen her from afar earlier in the day - she was beautiful then. Now, she was radiant. She glowed under the white dress, and a long braid was pulled over her shoulder and fell just below her chest. He marvelled at her and, for a moment, thought it fateful that the most beautiful woman he'd laid eyes on was walking down the aisle to him. But she did not want him. He pushed his desires back in his mind and tore his eyes away from her.

~

The man she'd seen on the balcony was Laird Carrigan; she was right. He stared at her as she started down the aisle. His gaze moved up and down her body, filling Darra with nervous fear. She couldn't stop her mind from wandering and imagined him leading her to his chamber to have his way with her after.

As she approached the arch at the end of the aisle, her betrothed looked away from her. She felt a strange sense of relief and self-doubt wash through her. *Am I not fair enough to keep his attention?* she thought as she continued, her cheeks flush. She suddenly became aware of every muscle in her body and tightened them to control them fully. Every step closer, she felt herself growing annoyed. Who did he think he was to be unhappy with her? He was lucky to be marrying someone like her.

She stood across from him, and he stuck both hands in front of him for her to take. She cautiously took his hands as he looked down at her, standing a foot taller with a clenched jaw. Darra hadn't expected him to be so handsome. She felt odd looking at him and admiring his features. Yet, even with his jaw tightly shut and his eyes averting her, she found something about him to be charming. Perhaps it was the stubble growing on his face or the laugh lines in the corner of his eyes - something she'd known few people to have since the war began.

She allowed herself to admire his features for a moment, then the moniker "Samuel the Cruel" surfaced in her mind, and she thought perhaps the creases at the corners of his eyes formed as he laughed at the slaughter and misfortune of her people. She took a deep breath and focused her attention on the priest. He slowly read through their marriage rights and paused to look at them both for a moment. Darra had attended several weddings in the Sloane clan and knew he was about to ask them to share the vows they'd written for each other. But, unfortunately, she hadn't prepared any. She might have if she'd have been given some time after her arrival or perhaps gotten to interact with her new husband before their wedding.

"The Groom and the Groom's Bride shall now recite the vows they've written for one another." The old minister said with a slight nod towards them.

Laird Carrigan looked at Darra for a moment as she stumbled with her words. "I havenae had- I donnae" she kept whispering to them both, trying not to cause a scene.

"Skip them," Laird Carrigan said in a firm tone. The minister nodded his head. Darra saw his face blush as he stumbled into the next part of the speech. He spoke for a few minutes before declaring them married.

"Laird Samuel Carrigan, ye may now kiss ye'r bride."

Darra's body tensed, and she watched her new husband's jaw tighten even more as he slowly leaned down and kissed her lips. She was thankful it was quick. She hardly knew him and felt it might be awkward to have their first exchange be a sloppy kiss. She blushed when he pulled away from her and flashed him an uneasy smile that he did not return; he appeared to almost be in pain as if kissing her had been some form of torture for him. Finally, he let go of one hand and led her back down the aisle and out of the room.

This is it, Darra thought to herself. *He will lead me to his chambers and have his way with me.* Fear rushed through her limbs as they left the chapel, and he began walking her down an unfamiliar hall.

He thought hard and fumbled with words in his head but couldn't think of anything to say to Darra - his *wife*. He could sense her tension as he held her hand to guide her to the dining hall, confident she would now be stressing over her new title and how she would fare in the clan. Her hand was soft and delicate. He held it as gently as he could in his large rough-calloused hand. He didn't want to bother her by squeezing hers too hard, and he was admittedly too self-conscious about the rough calluses from training with a sword for so long.

The couple was met with the scents of savoury herbs and warm buttery bread as he opened the double doors to the dining hall. Standing around the long dining table were servants and some of his trusted advisors and old friends he'd fought with in battle. They all knelt and nodded their heads to him. He walked her to a raised dais at the back of the room and pulled the heavy iron chair out; she smiled and thanked him before sitting. *She has a marvellous smile,* he thought as he sat in his chair.

"Thank ye all. Ye may stand and sit. Enjoy this feast in our honour!" He said, and all the guests rose and sat in their chairs. Servants walked to the dais and set shining goblets down in front of him and Darra before pouring a sour-smelling wine into them both. Samuel hated wine, he'd much prefer to be drinking mead with his comrades at the long table, but familial tradition dictated he drink this wine with his wife on the first night of their union. He lifted his goblet towards Darra, and she gently tapped the rim of her glass on his before they took a drink.

The guests all reached across the table to fill their plates with delicious turkey and freshly baked pieces of bread, and the servants brought plates too and from the dais full of the same. Samuel watched Darra gingerly pick at her food and watch the crowd of people. The servants' occasional "congratulations" came as they refilled her wine glass, and she nodded in thanks, though he was sure she wasn't thankful for the union.

He wished it could have been different too.

~

Darra's head felt light as she continued to drink the wine. She nibbled some of the food to lessen the wine's effects, but her stomach was too queasy. It smelled fantastic and was genuinely delicious, but the idea of eating made her feel ill - she was beyond nervous. She knew she'd be expected to consummate her new marriage as soon as the dinner was through. In the eyes of the church, it wasn't official until the act of the consummation itself - and often, close family members would wait outside the room, ensuring the union was consummated. *Perhaps more wine will make it seem easier,* she thought as she swallowed more of the sour old wine.

She snuck glances at her husband when she thought he wasn't looking at her. There was no denying he was handsome, and she was thankful for that. But the more she noticed how broad his shoulders were and how the muscles on his arms strained against the fabric of his tunic, she felt nervous and took another sip of wine.

None of the guests approached her for the first half of dinner, and she was very thankful for that. During the second half, the only person she recognized, Angus, walked up to them with a small box in his hands. He handed it directly to Darra, and she smiled at him as she took it. He lingered for a few moments, and she realized she was supposed to open it. She lifted the top off the box, and inside was an ornate leather-bound book. Immediately curious about what it was, she lifted it carefully and pulled the cover open to see blank pages.

"I thought it might be nice for ye to have a place where ye can express ye'rrself without the fear of judgment, especially from those who do not know ye." He said to her with a nod. And before placing it back, she discovered a lovely writing set inside the box.

"How thoughtful. Thank ye very much, Angus. I will treasure this dearly." She smiled at him and carefully placed the box on the ground at her feet. It wasn't a lie in any way. Back home, she would often journal and document her daily thoughts. However, she hadn't brought her journal with her in fear someone might read it to discover her feelings about Callum or the harsh things she thought of her now-husband.

Shortly after Angus, several other guests approached the dais and brought the new couple some small tokens and gifts.

They received tea sets, vases, tapestries, fresh floral arrangements, and numerous tiny trinkets. She wasn't sure the purpose they served, but they were all ornately inscribed and decorated with tiny crystals and painted glass.

Towards the end of dinner, Darra watched a woman with long red hair that hung loose and flowed in waves well past her waist walk in, holding the hand of a yeng boy - she recognized them as the pair standing by Samuel at the ceremony. The woman approached the head table, and many guests took to whispering as soon as they saw her. Darra shivered as the woman approached the dais. It was as if a sudden draft had found its way deep within the keep. The woman stood before the couple and let go of the boy's hand. The child immediately ran around the dais to Samuel, who suddenly seemed happy for the first time today. The woman approached Darra and laid a bright orange flower in front of her.

"Welcome to the family Mrs. Sloane," she said in a cool tone before stepping down and glaring sharply at the child. The boy sighed and walked toward her, and they exited the room. Darra looked at Samuel; he seemed flustered by the woman's sudden arrival. After some time, Samuel cleared his throat and stood beside her. He looked down at her, and she stood too.

"Please, continue to fill ye'r bellies with the delicious food and mead we've prepared for ye all, but it is time for my bride and me to take our leave." His tone was flat, reluctant even - but the mood in the crowd changed. She blushed as drunken cooing rang through the dining hall and her new husband held out his hand for her to take.

She stumbled a bit as he walked her down from the dais, the wine seemed to rush through her body, and she felt she couldn't fully control her limbs. The chambermaids had warned her of drinking too much wine on an empty stomach, and she realized her mistake. A strong arm gripped her waist and steadied her as they walked out of the room and down the hall. It was Samuel's arm around her. She wanted to pull away, to tell him to take his hands off her, but couldn't find any words. She noticed he began leading her down a hall she was unfamiliar with - she was unfamiliar with the layet of the keep. *He must be taking me to his room!* She thought in a panic.

Sure enough, he opened the doors to a bedroom that was not hers; it was dark with a few candles lit on the bedside tables, the large windows all had their curtains drawn, and the scent of fresh roses filled the room. He walked her to the bed and sat her down on it, where she saw a dozen roses laid against the pillow. Her body was rigid, and she rested her hands on her lap. She couldn't meet his eyes - seeing the carnal lust in his eyes would undoubtedly frighten her more than anything.

He pulled his hand away just as she expected him to pounce on her. She was confused but filled with relief.

"They'll expect ye to sleep here, at least tonight," he said as he backed away from her and started walking towards a door at the side of the room, "ye'll be fine to go back to ye'r chamber tomorrow night. I'll be in my study tonight." He walked through the door without saying anything else to her.

~

Samuel left early the following morning. He was tired, having hardly slept during the night, and he found resting his head against his sizeable wooden desk wasn't very comfortable. But it was the best option since his new wife, a woman forced to be with him, needed to sleep in his room on their wedding night. So before leaving for the day, he placed a small letter on the nightstand that he hoped she'd see before leaving.

Yawning heavily and with bags under his eyes, he knew everyone he'd meet would assume he had been up all night with Darra consummating their marriage - and a large part of him wished he had, but not before giving her time to adjust. She seemed more than relieved when he walked away from her, so the thought of someday soon telling her they would need to try to conceive an heir made him nervous.

He walked down the long hallway from his room and down the stairs to meet Angus. He was to spend time during the dinner to gauge the reactions and feelings of the clan members and report to Samuel. Angus was facing the window and looking out at the lush green fields beyond. He turned to face Samuel as he shut the door.

"Morning, Laird. I trust ye had a bonne night," he said with a slight grin. Samuel flashed a smile back and nodded vaguely.

"A true gentleman doesnae speak of such things," he replied, brushing the suggestive dialogue aside. "Now, please tell me the people at dinner accepted my new wife with open arms."

"Actually," Angus started as he took a seat and rested his elbows on his small desk covered in papers, "her overall reception was quite good. She's quiet, and the clan noted it, but they understood she might have been overwhelmed. Nevertheless, she could have a real place here, and hopefully, she will warm up to accept it."

He was relieved, he had thought about what he'd have to do if the clan wouldn't accept her, and nearly all of the options would have resulted in war resuming and a significant retaliation from the Sloane clan.

Darra had woken late in the day, the curtains were still drawn, but through the sheer white, she could tell the sun was high in the sky. It took her a moment to look around the room and realize where she was. She found a piece of paper folded on the nightstand by her and picked it up; it was a letter from her new husband.

> Dear Mrs. Sloane,
>
> I suppose I should say Carrigan now?
>
> This union, as ye well ken, was a peace arrangement. I suggested it to ye'r father as I grew tired of watching a pointless war ravage my home. I ken if ye need time to adjust before accepting ye'r role as my wife and the Lady of the Carrigan Clan. Though we've not spoken at great length, I am excited to ken more about ye. I find a natural curiosity and thirst for knowledge and adventure in ye'r eyes; we can learn quite a bit from each other. I trust that in time ye will forgive me for taking ye from ye'r home.
>
> P.S. - It would be prudent not to discuss our marital affairs with anyone yet, as I do not wish for our marriage to be claimed as false.
>
> Samuel

*A*s she finished reading the letter, she looked around the room at his belongings and felt a strange warm endearment towards him. Last night she had been frightened of him, she'd convinced herself to hate him even, but this letter now shed light on a kinder, more generous side of him that she could come to appreciate. He appeared rugged and closed off, but even taking the effort to write such a thing for her proved he might be decent.

She left the room in her wedding attire. She realized what the people she passed would think, but in a way, she didn't care. Samuel suggested they keep their current state a secret, and what better way than to walk from his chamber to her own in yesterday's clothes. People would undoubtedly believe they'd shared a passionate night, and she felt shame in that but a strange sense of pride, too. If the people thought they were *genuinely* married, that would mean an end to the war. No more lives lost, no more families ruined, no more carnage - normally, she'd hate to lie, but this one was justified.

She'd crossed paths with a few people on her way to her chamber, two of which were Keiren and Kailee. They'd been waiting in the hall for her to arrive to help her begin her day. Upon seeing her, they both looked at each other and giggled. Then, they faced her, arms tucked behind their backs, expecting to hear every detail.

She smiled warmly, and they followed her into her room. Keiren began drawing a bath for her, and Kailee brought in a tray of biscuits and tea for her to nibble while waiting. Darra eagerly began eating the biscuits, they were no longer warm and had become slightly chewy from the long wait, and she got them down with some tea.

During her bath, she couldn't stop thinking about the letter her husband had left for her. For the first time, she did think he could be a nice man. But, for them to become friends, they'd have to speak to one another. She laughed softly to herself as an idea popped into her head. *I'll send him a letter, too. An invitation!* She thought and hurried from the tub to sit at her writing desk.

~

After the meeting with Angus, Samuel returned to his room to rest. It had been a long night in his study, and he needed to sleep desperately. He'd told Angus and some of the servants who typically waited on him that he had a headache and to leave him for the night. When he got to his room, he found a small sealed envelope slid under his door. He picked it up and saw his name written in a delicate script. He opened it and smiled shortly after reading the first few words.

Dear Laird Carrigan,

I suppose I should say husband now?

I understand why the union was arranged, and I harbour no ill feelings about it. Thank ye for allowing me the time to adjust. This has all been quite overwhelming. From the brief time I've been here, I see a place for myself, and hopefully, I can adjust to it soon enough. I do have quite the appetite for adventure! I've been dreaming of exploring the woodlands since I first saw them. Perhaps someday, ye can walk through them with me, and we can find commonalities.

> *In the meantime, I find communicating through writing rather dull. So I would be pleased if ye would join me for dinner tonight.*
>
> *ye'r wife, Darra*

She's clever; he thought when he finished reading through her invitation. He looked out the window and saw the sun still high in the sky. He had plenty of time to rest his head before dinner.

∽

*D*arra waited by herself for an hour in the dining hall before deciding to leave for the night. *Perhaps he hadn't seen the letter?* As she slowly walked back to her room, she couldn't help but feel rejected.

*S*amuel woke with a sigh as he realized the sun was rising. *I missed dinner* was the first thing he thought that morning. It was a kind gesture of her to invite him, and he had slept through the meal! He might have ruined any chance they'd have at forming an amicable connection. He scolded himself over it in the bath that morning while he tried to think of any way he could make things up to her.

Unfortunately, he wouldn't have the time that day. His stepmother, Shannon, had requested his council that day, and he would have to spend god knows how long listening to her bicker. He knew she'd be in the library shortly after breakfast waiting for him. *What could she possibly want to talk about?* So he thought as he dressed for the day.

He was nice enough to let her stay in his keep after his father passed away, and he now had to listen to her constant complaints and derogatory remarks at him. She would constantly find a nerve with him and strike at it repeatedly. He dreaded any encounter with her.

Before leaving for the library, he drank his morning tea and ate a bowl of porridge. Of course, Shannon waited for him in the center of the room, standing behind an oversized plush chair. Usually, he'd find reprieve in his library - a quiet escape from the rest of the keep. Here he could open a book and learn about old clans and lands far away. If he had the choice, he'd spend most of his days here with the books. But seeing Shannon's scowl tainted the air of this normally inviting room.

"Ye've finally arrived," she said as she plopped down in the chair.

"What do ye want, Shannon?" Samuel asked, his voice filled with impatience.

"I was just wondering if ye've had a chance to tell ye'r bride about her brother yet?" A sick smile crept across her face as she lowered her head to chuckle at Samuel.

"Donnae ye dare say anything-"

"Why, I'm offended ye'd think I would! I would hate for her to find out from one of the servants."

"What is it ye want? Certainly, ye wouldnae be threatening me without some selfish motive," Samuel retorted. Anger rose to his face and flushed his skin every time she sighed and shook her head as if she were innocent of these games.

"What I wanted was stolen from me when she arrived at the clan, and I donnae think ye'll be able to fix it anymore." She rose from her chair and exited the room. *This was a warning,*

Samuel thought to himself, and he paced back and forth for what felt like hours, trying to figure out the best way to move forward.

∼

*D*arra spent the late morning exploring the keep. She was only familiar with her room, and if she was to make this her home, she might as well get to know the walls and the decorations lining them, the people working within them, and the sprawling fields and gardens beyond them.

She started in the kitchen. That was closest to the dining hall, which she had already known well enough. There she met a friendly older cook named Orla. She had a kind face and a warm, cheerful laugh - she was the type of person she knew she'd be able to come to with any trouble and feel reassured instantly. After that, she explored the guest rooms and some of the common areas in the castle. There was a luxurious parlour where she found Angus lounging while reading some documents - the furniture was plush and soft, but she could tell it was old and hardly used. *There are hardly any signs of life on these!* She thought as she traced her fingers on the fabric. Darra thought back to her old home, the furniture worn down through years of hosting gatherings for their friends and even some of the servants (who had felt more like family to them).

She admired the old tapestries, delicate vases and trinkets, hand-drawn maps, and precious heirlooms she passed as she explored. She finally discovered the room she was most looking forward to; the library. She'd read through nearly every volume at her old library and couldn't wait to see what the Carrigan clan had collected over the years for her to read now that she was one of them.

Samuel stood at the end of the room, staring out the window. When the door opened, he turned around. He was surprised to see her.

"Hello," Darra said after a moment of them staring at one another. He nodded at her without saying a word. "I was waiting for ye last night in the dining room."

"I'm sorry, I just-" he fumbled to find the words. He didn't want to seem like a fool for falling asleep but didn't want Darra to think he purposefully ignored her. "There's no excuse, really. I should have been there. I apologize." She nodded at him in response and walked further into the room. She scanned the tall shelves and delicately traced her fingers over the spines of the books; hyperaware Samuel was watching her all the while.

"Ye've got quite a bonnie collection," she said in awe of the enormous amount of books.

"Well, it's ye'rs now, too," he replied with a small laugh and a smile. That was the first time she'd heard him laugh, and she enjoyed the sound of it very much.

"What would ye recommend I start with then?" She stood right in front of him and looked up at his face. When she spoke, he looked down at hers. They were very close together. Darra usually felt nervous, and she was surprised to discover she didn't; the feeling was instead replaced with excitement.

"As the newest addition to the Carrigan clan, perhaps some reading on *our* family's history?" Samuel replied. *That's right, our family. How strange,* Darra thought after hearing the emphasis on the word.

"That sounds splendid. Ye'll have to choose the best starting point for me," she paused for a moment and looked at him again, "I hate to ask a second time. I certainly don't wish to nag ye if ye can't, but would ye -"

"It would be an honour," Samuel said before she could finish her sentence, "in fact, I'll host the dinner. The view from my balcony is stunning. Come to my room at sunset, and we'll dine there." Darra nodded and smiled. She felt her cheeks flush as she gave him a small curtsy and left the room.

She rushed back to her room and rummaged through her clothes to find something fitting to wear.

∽

Sunset couldn't come fast enough, Samuel thought as he rearranged the tableware on the small round table on his balcony for the tenth time. *Everything needs to be perfect*, he thought and did another walk-through of his room to ensure it was immaculate and ready for company.

He was only planning on having dinner with Darra tonight, nothing else. He did not want her to think he was using this as a gateway to bedding her. Although, the thought of doing just that crossed his mind a few times in the hours leading up to dinner. He pushed it out of his head and tried to focus on anything else.

Just as the sun began to set, a slight knock came from his door. He opened it to find Darra in a gorgeous silk dress with floral embroidery. The soft green colours made her eyes brighter and perfectly accentuated her hair. He smiled, gestured for her to come in, and then led her to the balcony. He pulled her seat out and poured her a glass of wine before he poured himself one.

He sat across from her in awe for a moment before he could say anything. There were no words to capture how beautiful she was sitting there across from him, the fading sun reflected off her porcelain skin, revealing soft brown freckles, and her hair looked like a flame in the way it absorbed the rays of sunshine and the highlights danced freely. But the most captivating part was her eyes; the green was liquid, and flecks of brown and gold moved within it like sand shifting in an emerald ocean.

"This is a bonnie view," Darra finally said after a few moments sitting there. She sipped her wine and smiled at him.

"Aye, It certainly is," he said, still staring at Darra. "I'm glad ye'r here. I wanted ye to see the true beauty of the grounds."

They sat in silence for a moment, but they soon found a rhythm for communicating with each other. Orla brought them a delicious roasted chicken with potatoes and boiled vegetables, and they both savoured the meal and discussed some of their favourite foods. Samuel noted that blueberry cobbler was her favourite food, and she had a love of desserts in general.

By the end of supper, they were well acquainted with each other. Both laughed, smiled at one another, and listened intently to the other's stories of things they'd experienced as children. Samuel consciously avoided speaking of things that happened during the war to avoid seeming brutish.

After they dined, Samuel walked to the edge of the balcony and rested his elbows, looking out at the land below. Darra followed and did the same. They stood together in silence, which they found to be comfortable, and admired the land. Darra pointed out a few constellations in the sky and told him the stories behind them, and he smiled at her the entire time she stared towards the heavens with a broad smile and a twinkle in her eyes.

She looked back at him when she was through to see a peaceful look on his face, his eyes were half-closed as he stared at her, and an endearing smile rested on his lips. Darra felt strongly about what she wanted at that moment and inched closer to him. She was excited to see he followed her step and moved closer to her. They stood beside each other, mere inches apart, with magnetic energy forming between them.

Samuel held her face in his hands and leaned down to kiss her. She opened her mouth to his and kissed him back as she placed her small hand on his broad chest and slowly raised it to trace over his neck and land on his jaw. He pulled her close, and the couple kissed passionately; time felt like it had stopped for them both.

They were finally interrupted when a small voice yelled below them. The couple broke off their embrace to see Shannon storming towards the keep with her son following close behind, yelling for her to slow down.

A sinking feeling came through Samuel as he wondered if she'd seen their kiss.

*D*arra practically floated back to her room. She was so happy she felt as if she weighed nothing at all. She opened the door and fell backwards on her bed. She softly traced her fingers over her still tingling lips. She could see a future with this man, she already knew she would have one, but now she could see a *happy* future with him - one full of love, passion and warmth. She was about to undress and get ready for bed when a loud knock came on her door.

She slowly walked over and opened it to see Shannon. They hadn't had a formal interaction since the wedding dinner when she'd given her the lily, but Samuel told Darra all about her during supper. She was his father's new wife. They'd married just a few years before he passed away, and Shannon had given him a new heir. From the brief interaction with her at dinner, and the tiny bit of information Samuel gave her, she sensed a dark aura around her - something wasn't quite right, but she couldn't put her finger on what exactly.

Shannon pushed into the room and faced Darra with a sharp intensity in her eyes.

"Listen close, child, the man ye'r married to, is a monster," Shannon started saying. Darra hung her mouth open, unsure what to say or if she should say anything. "Ye think he earned the title Samuel the Cruel for no reason? He's a killer. He was *raised* from birth to be a killer, and I wouldnae put it past him to have some evil goal ye'r nay aware of." She paused and watched Darra struggle to find words. An evil smile grew on her face and she shook her head back and forth. "Donnae believe me? Just ask ye'r brother."

"What do ye mean?" Darra asked, a new indignant fire raging inside her at the mention of her late brother.

"Wait, ye cannae, can ye?" Shannon said with faux sorrow in her voice. "He's dead and ye'r husband killed him." Darra shook her head no and backed away from Shannon slowly, stumbling as she blindly walked into furniture. Shannon looked down the hall behind her and laughed softly to herself. "Why, here he comes now, how about ye ask him ye'rself."

As if on cue, Samuel appeared in the doorway. The worry on his face grew stronger as he took in the situation.

"Shannon! What are ye doing here, we've been looking for ye," Samuel said breathlessly.

"I think ye two have something to discuss!" She replied in an all too chipper tone before turning on her heels and leaving the room.

Darra stared at Samuel in shock, trying to muster the courage and words to confront him.

"Are ye okay, Darra?" Samuel asked her. He walked towards her and reached for her face. She slapped his hand away; a part of her savoured the hurt that filled his face.

"Is it true?" She whispered to him angrily. He shook his head as if he didn't understand what she was asking. "Did ye kill him? Tell me now!" She yelled at him, each word filled with heartbreak and disdain.

"Darra, I-" he stumbled with words and reached out to touch her shoulder.

"Tell me the truth, damn it!" Tears welled in her eyes and streamed down her face. He didn't need to say anything. She could see it. Laird Samuel 'The Cruel' Carrigan - her husband - had killed her brother.

"Aye, I did," he started to say, "it isnnae something I'm proud of. Darra, I was going to tell ye I just didnae ken how."

"ye'r a coward," she spat at him, her words full of venom. He shook his head and reached out for her again, and she pushed his hands away before running out of the room.

She sped down the halls and ran down the stairs to get to the front door of the keep. She swung the doors open and rushed barefoot through the soft green grass. It was dark, and she didn't know where to run, but she kept moving. The cold air was refreshing as it brushed against her skin, flushed with rage. She only stopped running when her lungs burned so intensely that she couldn't stand another step forward.

Woods surrounded her, she didn't even remember crossing into the dense brush or jumping over twigs and logs, but her bare feet felt the damage now that she had stopped. Finally, exhausted, she found a fallen tree covered in brown mushrooms and moss and leaned against it. After some time, Darra cooled down and realized she was freezing. She shivered and rubbed her shoulders to try and make warmth.

Shelter. She would need to find some sort of shelter for the night. She scoured the dense trees hoping to find an old cabin or even a cave where she could seek refuge from the elements. She moved deeper into the woods to find something but quickly realized she would have no luck.

She was alone out here and likely to freeze to death come morning. *If I make it until morning anyway,* she thought as she looked around. A twig snapped behind her, and she quickly turned around. A large white wolf, growling with hungry eyes, had just found its supper.

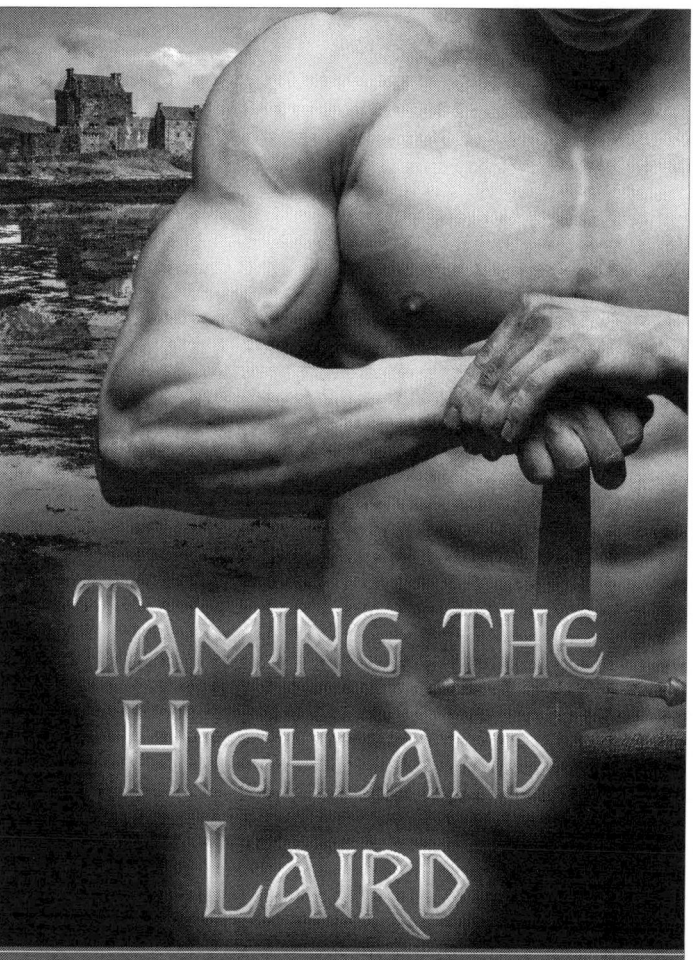

TAMING THE HIGHLAND LAIRD

*D*arra had been missing from the Carrigan keep for over an hour. It was late. Samuel worried she would soon succumb to the elements. Though the day had been beautiful, the night would often drop to freezing. His worry rose when he thought of the wolves and bears hungry after a long hibernation. He tried pushing those thoughts to the back of his mind; standing on the balcony, he watched the edges of the woods for any sign of his wife.

"That's it," he said, storming into the room to dress in his riding clothes and ready himself for a trip into the woods. He walked into the small library where Angus was awake, waiting for any word of Darra's whereabouts. "Angus, I'm gonae to search for her myself. Send some riders out to search as well." Angus didn't have a chance to respond before he left the room.

He went to the stables, hopped on his horse, and pressed his heels into her side to take off, rushing across the moist green hills to the woods where he thought Darra might have entered. He confirmed by footsteps in the underbrush that someone, he hoped it was her, had been walking through recently.

Just as he'd begun tracking her footsteps through the woods, he stopped and looked around feverishly as he heard a shrill scream from deeper inside the woods.

"Darra," he said aloud and took off towards the scream.

~

*D*arra froze in place, unsure of how to proceed. *If I run, it will chase me and outrun me. But if I stay here, it will undoubtedly devour me,* she thought, slowly backing away from the wolf. It inched closer to her with every step she took. She kept her eyes on the beast, readying herself for it as she watched drool drip from its snarled mouth.

The wolf then pounced, and she dove to the side. A scream escaped her as the ground collapsed under her foot, and she went tumbling into a small ditch. She stood as quickly as possible, the wolf descending the small hill towards her. Darra ran through the woods, but the wolf soon caught her. She screamed again as she was knocked to the ground from behind.

She rolled onto her back and stuck her hands up just in time to stop the wolf from biting her neck. Ominously, it loomed over her, snapping at her, unable to sink its teeth into her. She felt her muscles wavering under the weight of the beast. "Help!" she screamed into the dark empty woods praying someone would save her.

The wolf bit her arm, and she cried out in pain, realizing it could very quickly kill her at any second. The wolf cried out in pain and released her arm from its mouth. It fell to the ground beside her, quietly whimpering as it bled out into the dirt. She stared at the creature in shock, confused about what had happened. Darra looked up to see Samuel standing over her with a sword in his hand, and small blood spatter on his white tunic.

She saw his lips moving but could not hear a word come from his mouth. Instead, all she heard was a sharp ringing. She reached her hand to the back of her head and felt a small wet spot that was warm and sticky. She pulled her hand to the front of her face and saw blood on her fingertips.

Samuel knelt in front of her and extended a hand to her. She ignored it and tried to stand on her own. Darra slowly made it to her feet and felt herself teetering over. She was falling, but before she hit the ground, she felt a pair of strong arms catch her. She looked up to see Samuel's face hanging over hers. The trees began to pass her as he carried her to his horse.

She closed her eyes and went to sleep.

~

I cannae believe I let this happen to her, Samuel thought as he carried his delirious and injured wife through the dark woods. Then, reaching his horse, he carefully lifted Darra onto it and hopped on behind her, holding her tightly.

He began riding back to the keep. When he saw others on the way, he yelled to them that she was safe now, and they quickly informed all the other people who had taken off into the woods to search. As soon as he arrived, he carried her into the keep and rushed her to her bed. Calling out to anyone who could hear him; find Janice, the keep's healer, and send her to Darra's room. Shortly after he laid her in her bed, a small stout woman with long gray hair arrived with a large bag containing bandages, salves, splints and numerous other items he couldn't identify.

"What happened to her arm?" She said, quickly pulling a needle and thread from the bag alongside some vials of liquids and a tin with cream inside of it.

"A wolf was biting her arm when I found her. And I think she's hit her head too," Samuel said, gently lifting her head to reveal a bloody patch at its back.

"Ye'd best go to your room and rest, this will take some time, and I donnae want any distractions as I patch her up," Janice said as she started pouring some liquid into a vial and dabbing it on her arm. Samuel nodded and quietly left the room.

Two days after encountering the wolf, Darra woke in her bed covered in bandages. Rays of sunshine snuck through the drawn curtains of her room, filling it with dim light. The bedside candle flickered as she sat up to look around, unsure of what had happened to her. She heard rustling beside her bed, quickly turning to see what caused it. Her head ached when she moved. Samuel sat in a plush chair beside her bed, waiting for her to wake up. Gently, he reached for her hand and held it. She watched his eyes assess her bandaged wound with a deep sense of concern behind them.

"What happened?" she asked him after a moment, recalling the events leading up to this.

"Ye were," Samuel paused, hesitating to find the right words, "a wolf attacked ye." Darra stared at him in shock, shaking her head back and forth in denial. Then, before she could speak, an image of a wolf snarling on top of her flashed before her eyes. Quickly following was everything else leading up to it; rushing through the woods, Samuel confessing to killing her brother in combat, Shannon coming to her and telling her about it, and the kiss she had with him just before. She stared at Samuel for a minute and pulled her hand away from his.

"How did ye do it?" Darra asked him while he turned away. Samuel thought to himself, then sighed as he realized what she was asking.

"I donnae want to upset ye right now. Ye're very injured," he sputtered, seemingly desperate to avoid the subject as long as possible.

"Figures ye'd try and keep it from me," she stood from her bed and walked to the windows, opening the curtains wide. Bright daylight flooded the room, temporarily blinding her. She stumbled back from the light. Before moving too far, Samuel was behind her guiding her back to the bed.

"When ye've recovered, I'll tell ye everything. Answer any question. But right now, ye need to rest. Ye took a blow to the head, and this cannae be good for it," he said, helping her to bed, careful not to hurt her arm. "I'll fetch Janice to check up on ye now that ye're awake."

She rested her head against her pillows and waited quietly in her room. A few minutes after Samuel left, a small woman with long gray hair entered her room without knocking.

"Ye're Janice, I take it," Darra said as she approached her bedside.

"Aye, we havenae formally met yet. If only it had been under better circumstances," Janice responded with a small laugh. She reminded her of her mother, and Darra was able to find comfort in that and relax a bit. Janice unwrapped her bandage and looked over her wound. Darra peaked at it when the dressing was off and saw a giant bite mark around her forearm. She gasped and quickly looked away.

"I was hoping it was a dream or a lie," Darra said, focusing on the vase of roses, wincing as Janice cleaned the bite and began wrapping new bandages over it.

"I ken ye're angry with him, but if Samuel hadnae gotten to ye in time, we would likely still be piecing together body parts right now," Janice said. The more she thought about the attack she felt sick to her stomach.

If it weren't for him, I wouldnae be in this position in the first place, Darra thought to herself as Janice finished patching her up. She quickly examined her head, ensuring Darra could see and hear properly before tying a small bandage around her head to cover the wound on the back.

"I want ye to stay rested until tomorrow night. We'll have your meals sent up until then. So ye get comfortable and try to relax. Aye?" Janice said as she packed all of her medical tools away. Darra nodded her head and thanked her before she left. When Janice opened the door to go, Darra noticed Samuel waiting outside her room, leaning against the wall beside the door. She barely heard him ask Janice how she was fairing before the door shut.

A few hours passed, and her chambermaids, Kailee and Keiren, walked into her room carrying a food tray. They both looked over her nervously as they approached, and they made eyes at each other before saying anything to Darra. Kailee, who Darra had come to recognize as always having her red hair tied back in a low ponytail, carried the tray to her bed and set the legs of it down over her legs. She inhaled the scent of a rich soup full of savoury herbs and fresh vegetables.

"Thank ye, Kailee. I'm starving," she said as she brushed her hair behind her ears and picked up her spoon. She didn't take the time to savour the flavours but quickly ate the soup and finished a small bread loaf that had accompanied it. Kailee and Keiren watched her, both hesitating to ask questions, but Darra could see the curiosity on their faces.

"How are ye feeling?" Keiren finally managed to ask, looking down at her fingers, nervously tapping against the palm of her hand.

"I'm feeling fine. I have to rest here per Janice's instructions," she replied. She saw the twins look at one another as if there was something else they were hoping to coax out of her.

"That's good," Kailee replied with a pause, "we were all so worried for ye. Laird Carrigan didnae leave your bedside once while ye were asleep."

"Were ye truly bitten by a wolf?" Keiren interrupted and asked. Darra laughed and nodded at her. "We heard from Orla in the kitchen, who'd heard from the Fredericks, who had searched for ye, who saw ye carried back on a horse." She looked around as she spoke, ensuring she remembered the chain of events correctly.

"Word travels fast around here," Darra said, "I didnae realize people were searching for me." Guilt flooded her body as she imagined dozens of people from the keep searching for her in the cold night.

"Laird Carrigan had every man in the keep searching, and he sent word to the town to send aid too," Kailee said as she walked into the small privy and began preparing a bath for Darra, "he found ye before too many people were out, but everyone was happy to ken ye're safe now."

Darra soaked in the warm water for a while, thinking about the events leading up to her injuries and how she wouldn't be alive at that moment if it weren't for Samuel's timely rescue. *How kind they all searched for me,* she thought of the townsfolk with a slight smile. Finally, she got out of the tub and dried off before wrapping a thick robe around herself.

She opened the door to see Samuel sitting in the chair beside her bed again. He looked up at her in her robe and quickly averted his gaze. Darra laughed to herself when she saw the side of his face redden.

"Pardon me," he said towards the wall, "I owe ye an explanation. I intended to come here and give ye one. I apologize for intruding on ye." He turned and walked towards the door to her bedroom to take his leave, eyes firmly on the floor. Darra quickly rushed to the door and stood in front of it.

"Wait," she said, and he looked up from the ground to meet her eyes, "just tell me now. Please." He backed away and gestured for her to sit in one of the chairs. She sat across from him with her legs crossed, clutching her robe to ensure it was closed.

"Your brother died fighting," he started to say slowly, "he nearly cut off my head." He pulled down the top of his shirt and revealed a prominent scar under his neck. Darra gasped when she saw it. "He led a battle into the lands, and I led the defending army. Both of us fought hard, and the only reason I won over him was that he lost his footing on unfamiliar ground." He paused to let her take in the story. " Killing is nae something I've ever been proud of, but I defended my home and my people that day, and I donnae regret that." Darra wiped a tear from her eye and looked down at her lap.

"Ye must understand that I cannae forgive this right now," she said quietly.

"I understand completely," he replied, "perhaps someday we can move past it, but I donnae expect that to be anytime soon." He stared at her with deep melancholy and stood to leave the room. "For what it's worth, I am truly sorry. I wish it could have all been different." He walked to the door and left Darra sitting by the fire alone in a chair.

Samuel stormed through the keep searching in every room for his stepmother, Shannon. Eventually, he found her in a tower observatory room knitting. She scowled at him without saying a word when he entered.

"How dare ye intentionally try to ruin this for me - for the entire clan!" Samuel yelled at her. He stood right before her and looked at her with rage-filled eyes.

"Perhaps if ye'd have been clear with her from the beginning-" she started to say.

"I suppose that would be *my* business how I told her," he seethed at her, "and I planned to soon, but under different circumstances, perhaps one where she wouldnae have run off and nearly killed by a wolf!" He ran his fingers through his hair, pacing in front of Shannon.

"Surely ye're not blaming me for her immature reaction," Shannon said calmly, looking down at her lap to continue knitting as if the Laird of the clan wasn't reprimanding her. Her casual demeanour enraged Samuel; he ripped the knitting needle from her hands and tossed it over the balcony's edge.

"Why did ye do it?" He asked in a hushed voice. She sighed and shook her head as she bundled the thread in her hands. Then, she stood and faced Samuel directly.

"I despise ye," she whispered to him. "I always have. Every time ye went out to fight, I wished we'd soon learn that our enemies had killed ye *heroically* in combat." Samuel's eyes lit with anger, and he clenched his fist hard, he tried to breathe through his nose to calm himself, but rage coursed through his body, "My son should have been the new Laird, not ye. We would have never surrendered if it weren't for ye. Ye've made the entire clan look weak!"

"And ye'd see them all dead instead?" he said flatly. "Ye donnae understand the war. I do. I was raised to be a warrior, and I *am* a good one - we would have lost soon enough, and the Sloane clan would have taken over my lands. So, this marriage was truly the only option." He turned to leave the observatory. "Please remember I'm doing ye a courtesy by housing ye here. Donnae interfere with my marriage again," he warned her before he left.

⁓

*D*arra stood by her window and looked at the bright green hills waiting for the sun to set so she could leave her room. She started going stir-crazy that morning and desperately needed to see other faces and stretch her legs.

A slight knock came from the door, and she walked over to see who it was. Angus stood at the door, waiting for her. She smiled and greeted him kindly. He returned the gesture.

"Mrs. Carrigan," he said, waiting by the door. It took a moment to realize he was talking to her as she still wasn't used to hearing the title, "I thought I'd come and check on ye. Are ye hungry?" He asked her with a smile.

"How kind of ye, Angus. And I am famished," she replied. He extended his arm for her to grab, and she did. Then, he slowly walked her down the hallway, presumably to the dining hall for supper.

"How is your arm?" He asked her on the walk.

"It still hurts," she said, wincing as she extended her bandaged arm, "but it'll be fine soon. I wanted to talk to ye about possibly doing something to thank the townsfolk for searching for me." She explained to him an idea she had while waiting in her room earlier where she would throw a party for the townsfolk on the grounds of the keep to thank them for their help and allow Darra to get to know them properly.

"That would be a bonnie idea. I'll suggest it to Samuel if ye'd like," he replied just as they arrived at the dining hall. He escorted her to the dais and pulled her chair out for her to sit. She smiled and nodded her head at him to tell him to go forward with asking Samuel on her behalf.

She sat at the top of the dais, looking nervously at her lap as Samuel walked into the room. She took a deep breath and looked at him as he approached. *I have to keep it together around him in public, and I cannae let people see the distance between us,* she thought as she smiled at him while he walked towards his seat. He smiled back earnestly and sat down next to her.

A few kitchen staff came out and brought both plates of food and filled their cups with sweet wine. They ate their food in silence. Darra savoured a rich and creamy potato stew looking toward Samuel occasionally. After the meal, Samuel extended his hand for Darra to grab onto, she grabbed hold of it unenthusiastically, and he walked her out of the room. As soon as they were out of sight of the others in the dining hall, Darra pulled her hand away, walking ahead of him to go back to her chamber.

~

He couldn't blame her for being angry with him or hurt, but he felt frustrated with the situation. She would need time to forgive him, and he imagined it might take some time, but they had to keep up appearances so no one would question their union.

After dinner, he walked to his study and decompressed inside. *There must be something I can do to win her over,* he thought to himself, staring out the large window to the beautiful twilight beyond. A few ideas crossed his mind. The one he kept returning to was to purchase Darra a horse of her own - a gorgeous mare she could ride in the early mornings to see the beautiful lands she would now call home.

Samuel decided that would be his first gesture to win her over. He would leave for town early in the morning to find one of the best horses and bring it back for her. He tried to push the thought of her using the horse to ride back to the Sloane clan out of his mind but found the idea persisted in his head. *What if she rode back and told Laird Sloane I was responsible for his son's death?* He thought to himself. *That would resume the hostility between the clans, perhaps with more fervour than ever before.*

A knock came from the door, and Angus saw himself inside the study. He sat across from Samuel without saying a word.

"I ken very little about what was said to cause your fight with your new bride, but I'd suggest finding an end to it rather soon," Angus said after sitting in silence. Samuel laughed and shook his head at Angus.

"Aye, if only it were that simple," Samuel responded. He paused, then informed Angus of everything that happened. He laughed when Samuel proposed the idea of buying her a horse to make up for everything.

"I think the best option, for now, is to allow her to plan this event to thank the clan for joining ye in the search for her and possibly also turn it into a welcome event for her," Angus said, "perhaps ye can give her a horse during the event. But if we make her feel at home, she might be more likely to forgive." Samuel nodded and agreed with his advisor.

"I'll speak to her tomorrow and let her know she can start planning," Samuel said as he rose from his chair and walked out with Angus.

*D*arra lay in bed, unable to sleep for hours, thinking about what her brother must have experienced on the battlefield when he died. It was an odd comfort knowing that he put up a good fight and injured Samuel as much as he did. She couldn't help but wonder what things would be like if he'd have sent someone else to fight Samuel or if he'd have swung his sword just a bit harder and killed him. She knew she would have still been at the Sloane keep swapping scandalous tales with her younger sister, Deidre.

But the war would still be raging, she thought, *and more folk in my clan would die needlessly, or the Carrigans might have invaded and taken over.* She felt mixed emotions as she ruminated about the events. Part of her was furious with Samuel for ending her brother's life, knowing she could never forget that. But, on the other hand, another part of her realized dwelling on it would serve no good purpose, and she could not change past events. Was her brother's death the catalyst for the end of the war?

She knew that there would have been many more casualties had her brother not died, and she was thankful they now lived in peaceful times. She knew she would eventually have to accept that Samuel was the one who killed him, it would take time, but she knew it would be possible.

Samuel woke up to find a letter slipped under his door the following day. He recognized the delicate handwriting to be that of Darra's. He opened it without hesitation and read over her words.

Dear Samuel,
I would like to discuss some things with ye.

> *Perhaps over lunch. Please meet me in the garden at noon.*
>
> *Darra*

The letter came across as cold and informal. Darra must have quickly written it out overnight and slipped it under his door. But he was glad she reached out to talk because he would have to otherwise. Moreover, he began to feel that she might come around to forgiving him sometime sooner rather than later.

~

Darra put far too much effort into getting dressed, trying to appear as though she hadn't. She left a note for Samuel to meet her around noon for lunch, at which time she planned to propose the idea of the festival and hoped they could discuss financing it. She wanted to look like she didn't care to impress him, but she also wanted to look devastatingly beautiful, hoping it would soften him up to be willing to invest more money in her festival.

She wore an old blue floral gown her mother had gifted her years ago. It was one of her favourite dresses. It was light and breezy, comfortably form-fitting, and looked effortlessly regal. She tied her hair into a long braid and left for the kitchens shortly before she would need to arrive in the garden.

Orla was in the kitchen kneading a large piece of dough. She smiled at Darra when she walked in and wiped her hands on her flour-covered skirt. Darra asked her to prepare something simple for a picnic for her and Laird Carrigan, and she agreed to take it out to the garden at noon.

She then walked out to the garden and prepared an area for the two to dine in. Before long, noon was upon them, and she saw Samuel strolling towards the keep with a basket in hand. She waved at him from a distance, and he smiled and hurried toward her.

"Stay calm," she whispered as her limbs filled with numbing anger. She was angry with Samuel for keeping such an important secret. Would she have been able to move past this easier had she heard from his lips and not Shannon's? He approached her and set the basket down on Darra's small blanket on the ground.

"Orla stopped me on the way and told me to bring this out for us," he said, gesturing at the basket. Although Darra thought it was funny how he phrased that, Orla told him - the Laird of the clan - to bring it out, and he obliged. She knew he respected the people working in the keep, and his relationship with them intrigued her. She liked that he never tossed his title around and abused them like many in his position might be so inclined.

"Thank ye," she said and gestured to the blanket on the ground for him to sit down. He sat with his legs outstretched to the side, and she sat politely across from him with her legs crossed. They talked about the beautiful weather and the chirping birds and how good the food Orla prepared smelled.

"How is your arm?" Samuel asked her as he reached into the basket and pulled out some sliced chicken and vegetables. He watched her face as she looked down at her arm and instantly regretted asking. She looked distraught, like it was something she was trying to forget, and he brought it up to remind her.

"It's getting better. It still hurts a bit, though." She didn't elaborate any more than that. Samuel realized that such questions would remind her of the attack and all that had led up to it. The bite would serve as a reminder of her brother in some ways. "About that, I wanted to talk to ye about possibly throwing a thank-ye party, or a small festival, for the town.

I'm very appreciative that they all started searching for me, they don't even know me, and I'd like to repay them. What do ye think?"

"I think that's a bonnie idea," he quickly responded with a smile, "dark times have plagued the clan and giving them something to look forward to is a very kind gesture." Darra felt relieved to hear that. She assumed he would agree at the very least to try and smooth things with her. She never expected him to be enthusiastic about it, though.

"Thank ye!" She said with a genuine smile. Samuel watched her smiling and felt pleased to know she was happy. "I'd like to get started planning it right away. My chambermaids, Kailee and Keiren, would probably be happy to lend me a hand with it. About the cost," she started to say, but Samuel just shook his head and smiled.

"Donnae worry about that. Ye just plan it, and I'll take care of everything," Samuel said with a warm smile. Darra nodded and began telling him all about her vision for the event. Last night she'd been thinking of ideas, and she felt a garden party would be a fun theme for the day. Ideally, she would find some performers in town, a musician, someone who could juggle, acrobats etc. Samuel was able to name a few people he thought might be good performers for the event, and she eagerly wrote down their names and where she might find them.

"I think I'll go into town tomorrow and start planning. Thank ye so much for supporting this!" She grabbed his hand without realizing it, and he squeezed it gently. She slowly withdrew it from his and rested it in her lap. She sighed and took a deep breath preparing to say something.

"I'm sorry-" he started to say to her, but she quickly cut him off.

"I know. I've been thinking about everything constantly, and I just wannae to let ye know that I," she paused and looked at him with confused eyes, tears welling up inside of them, "I'm sorry, I'm just so torn on how I should feel right now." She took a moment to compose herself. Samuel looked at her as if he wanted to comfort her but was too afraid to touch her. "I understand what happened, and if it had happened differently, things could be much worse than they are now for everyone," she said as she wiped tears from her eyes, "it's impossible to forgive something like this, but I am willing to try."

Samuel was delighted. This was the best news he could have gotten today. He felt like jumping up and down and shouting his happiness to the world, but seeing how troubled Darra was with coming to a decision grounded him.

"Thank ye, that's more than I could have asked for," he said quietly. Darra began packing the picnic away, and Samuel helped her clean up. He carried the basket with the remaining food back to the kitchen for Orla to put away, then returned to his study to review some documents Angus had left for him.

Darra walked through the castle to find the twins to tell them about her new task and procure their help. She found them in the dining room polishing tableware alongside Orla. Darra sat down with all three of them, told them about the garden party she intended to throw, and asked them to spread the word about it and invite as many people as they wanted.

"I was hoping the two of ye could come into town with me tomorrow to invite people and find some performers," Darra said to the twins.

"We'd be thrilled to join ye," Kailee said quickly in response.

"It would be our pleasure, my lady," Keiren responded.

Darra directed the conversation to Orla to discuss food for the affair. Luckily, Orla was very passionate about cooking and was known in town for being quite the baker. She agreed to make a large cake for the event and some other treats but would need some kitchen hands to help cook for the entire clan. Darra agreed and put that on her list of things to look for when she went into town the next day.

Later that day, at dinner, Samuel and Darra sat side by side on their dais in the dining hall, smiling at one another, discussing ideas for the party Darra was so excited to be throwing. She was glad things were starting to feel normal for her; after the attack, she didn't think that would be possible, and it was a pleasant surprise.

Samuel stared at the letter on his desk for what felt like hours. A messenger from the Sloane clan arrived late morning to deliver it directly to him from Laird Sloane. His mind wandered, and he imagined dozens of things that could be within the envelope. He could be writing to declare war again. He might have heard she was injured and assumed the worst, given what happened to Darra. He could be questioning if there would be an heir on the way - the only proper way to have his marriage to Darra end the war for good. Or he could have just been writing to check in on his eldest daughter.

He thought of only one way to find out, tearing open the envelope. His heart sunk in his chest as he read over the words.

~

Darra woke early in the morning to get ready for her journey into town. This would be her first time seeing the town and most people living there. She purposefully dressed down, not wanting the townsfolk to feel like she thought she was better than them. She wore a simple green linen dress with a brown underbust corset with her hair undone in long waves reaching the center of her back.

She met Kailee and Keiren by the stables to depart for the day relatively early. The stable attendant helped her ready her horse for the short ride into town and quickly briefed her on the mare's temperament and how to gain her affection. Darra quickly found she liked this horse, it was calm and gentle, but she would have to earn its trust with careful treatment and kind gestures like petting and treats. She thought it was funny how the horse had such a strong will and respected the mare for it.

She and the twins rode into town, with the twins leading the way. It took less than half an hour to arrive in the town center, where a young boy rushed up to them and helped them off their horses before leading them into the stables.

"Where do ye two think is best to begin?" Darra asked the twins as she looked around and took in her surroundings. It was a small village; the buildings all sat very close to one another. In the center of the town, a small platform was erected, and it was deserted. It seemed very isolated to her compared to the village in her home clan. Even during the war, it was bustling with people moving around to sell wares and purchase goods. She and her sister would often sneak out of the keep to explore the town and spend time with the few friends they'd made in town.

She quickly realized why it was so dire her wedding took place so soon after her arrival. The war had destroyed this clan, it was much smaller than the Sloane clan, and with as many battles Darra remembered them being triumphant in, it must have been devastating to the Carrigans. She felt sorry for the people killed during the war as she walked through the quiet town, her footsteps a loud reminder of the pain they had all suffered. At that moment, she was glad to have been arranged to marry Samuel, they would have their problems, but she was happy to help bring about the war's end.

"We should try Matilda's bakery," Keiren said as they walked towards the town center.

"Aye, lead the way, then," Darra said to her with a smile. She watched the twins laugh and walk towards a small building with smoke from the chimney. She didn't know the twins well but couldn't recall them mentioning anything about family. She wondered if they had lost anyone during the war. She imagined they might have with it being such a small town.

They made it inside the bakery, where a middle-aged woman with short dark hair stood behind a flour-covered counter kneading dough. The twins walked up to the counter with eager smiles, and the woman greeted them. Keiren turned and gestured to Darra to come to the counter with them.

"This is Mrs. Darra Carrigan, Laird Carrigan's new wife," Keiren said with a smile. Darra stuck her hand out to shake the woman's hand. She smiled and dusted flour off her hands before shaking.

"Pleasure to meet ye, m'lady. I'm Matilda," she said in a soft lilt of a voice, "but I bet ye already guessed that. So sorry to hear what happened to your arm there. Those wolves are quite dangerous."

"Trust me, I ken," she said with a laugh and waved her bandaged arm. Matilda laughed with her and nodded her head.

"Ye're a funny one. I like that," she said and pointed at Darra. She blushed and smiled in response. The whole building smelled heavenly, and she inhaled the scent of fresh bread with a sigh.

"I must buy whatever I'm smelling here now," Darra said to Matilda. She nodded and walked to the back of the building, wrapped a fresh loaf of bread in parchment, and brought it to the counter for Darra. Darra reached for her coin purse to pay, but Matilda shook her head.

"Consider this a belated wedding gift," she said with a smile and handed her the still-warm bread. Then, Darra started telling her about her plan to throw a party for the town. Matilda was happy to be invited to the party and agreed to come to the keep early to help Orla, an old friend, prepare the food for the party.

As they were leaving the bakery, a young man the twins both recognized entered behind them. They looked at each other, blushing as he passed them. Darra smiled and bumped Keiren on the shoulder playfully.

"Who was that?" Darra asked both of them since it appeared they both had a slight crush on him.

"That's Daniel," Kailee whispered to her with a beet-red face, "he's so braw; every woman in town is in love with him." Keiren peeked inside the window to catch another glimpse of him as the young man bought his baked goods. Darra found her list of things to do, where she scribbled the names of a few people Samuel suggested to perform.

"He wouldnae happen to play the lyre, would he?" Kailee and Keiren both looked at her and nodded their heads. "I think Samuel suggested him as a performer at the party."

"Are ye gonnae to invite him?" Kailee said in an excited tone. Darra nodded, and the twins stared at each other with huge smiles. Then, they waited for a few minutes for him to come outside the bakery.

Darra waved at him to stop him. The twins blushed and walked back into the bakery to leave her alone with Daniel.

"Hello, I am Lady Carrigan," she started saying quickly. She felt embarrassed to introduce herself that way. "My husband and I will be throwing a party for the town and looking for performers. Laird Samuel said that he ken ye played the lyre well, and we were hoping ye could perform." He was very handsome. She could see why the twins were so fond of him. He had wavy blonde hair and striking blue eyes. She looked past him into the bakery to see the twins eagerly watching her.

"It's truly my pleasure to make your acquaintance, m'lady," he said softly, "Matilda was just telling me all about the party. I would be honoured to perform for ye." He smiled at her, and she felt her heart skip a beat. She felt guilty admiring him this way now that she was married, so she rushed away from him after giving him all of the information he needed.

~

He read the letter one more time to ensure he was reading it correctly. *Laird Guthrie Sloane is coming here,* he thought with dread. The letter read:

Dear Laird Samuel Carrigan,

It has come to my attention that my daughter has suffered a serious injury since being in your care. Therefore, out of concern for her safety, I will be travelling to your keep within the coming days to ensure Darra is safe and in the care of a decent man. Ye can expect fifteen of us, including myself and my youngest daughter, Deidre.

Laird Guthrie Sloane

Samuel didn't have to think hard to determine who told Laird Sloane about Darra's injuries. He folded the letter and stormed through the keep to find Shannon. She sat outside in the garden reading a book alongside his half-brother, Duncan, playing in the dirt.

"Duncan, can ye please run along? I need to have a word with your mother," Samuel said as he stood over Shannon with the letter in his hand. She smiled and chuckled to herself.

"Is that for me?" She asked in an all too calm tone. " I've been expecting a letter for a few days now."

"How could ye do this? It could mean the war resuming if Laird Sloane doesnae think she's safe here," he said to her in a hushed tone.

"Perhaps she isnae safe here. After all, she is married to the man who killed her very own brother." She laughed to herself some more. "Do ye think Guthrie is aware ye killed his heir?"

"What do ye want?" He asked through gritted teeth. He would not stand for her blackmailing him.

"I deserved to be the lady of the clan, and I was. Then that was taken from me by some wretch from the enemy clan. I will not just let her take over these lands. I had to work for this-"

"Ye worked for nothing!" Samuel yelled at her. He took a deep breath and tried to calm himself. "*I* trained and fought for these lands. My father did the same as his father before him. All ye did was seduce a widower. *Ye* have nae claim to these lands, and ye nay'er will." She closed her book and stared up at him with eyes full of hatred and determination.

"Ye've insulted me for the last time," she said as she gathered her things to leave.

"Ye've threatened me for the last time, do it again, and I'll have ye sent to live off in the woods by yerself." He turned and walked back to the keep, thinking of any way he could rid himself of Shannon.

∽

Darra returned to the keep after speaking to several people in the town about attending the party and possibly performing or helping in the kitchen. She opened her door to see a folded note on the floor asking her to meet Samuel in his study.

She knocked on the door to his study, and he quickly walked over and opened the door for her.

"Have a seat," he said and gestured to a chair across from his large desk. She was instantly worried about what he would say by his demeanour.

"Is everything alright," she asked in a concerned tone.

"It will be. Here, take a look at this." He handed her the folded-up letter and watched her face as she read the words. He was worried she might see this as an opportunity to leave and return home if her father deemed him too brutish or inappropriate for her. She furrowed her brow as she read, clearly wondering how he could have known about the injury, but by the end, she was smiling.

"My sister is coming to visit," she said, completely thrilled, "I've missed her so much!"

"I know ye have, but we need to discuss your father," he said seriously. "Ye know I've come to like ye, and yer father proposed our marriage entirely to bring an end to the conflict. But unfortunately, someone sent him a letter telling him ye were hurt, so he is already suspicious that I'm a monster.". "I cannae tell ye what to say to him, but I hope ye'll keep the war in mind." He felt dirty saying that as if he were blackmailing his wife somehow.

"Of course, I will," she responded quickly. She thought of the devastated town she'd visited earlier that day and how much the entire clan needed a break from the violence and time to recover. "The war resuming is the last thing I wannae see. I willnae say anything to risk that." She reassured him with a severe look in her eyes. She paused to find the words to describe what she felt. "When I was in town earlier, I saw what the war has done here. I see why our marriage happened, and I'm delighted about it. These people need to be happy again. This clan needs to be filled with life again," she paused and blinked fast to keep tears from welling in her eyes. She wanted so badly to transform this clan and give it life again. Saying it aloud made her realize how much she cared.

"What's the matter," Samuel said as he walked around his desk to comfort her. He leaned against the desk and placed a hand on her shoulder. She just took a deep breath and calmed herself down to compose herself.

"Thank ye. I'll be fine. I promise to speak to my father and straighten this out." They said their goodbyes, and she left to go to her bedroom

∽

Or us, Samuel thought as he replayed their conversation in his head. He slept that night sounder than he'd slept in quite a while. Was Darra on the verge of forgiving him? He felt as if they could be *partners* after all.

The letter said they'd be arriving in a matter of days; unfortunately, it didn't give an exact day or time, so they never knew when to be prepared for the Sloane clan's arrival. Darra spoke to the keep staff and had them prepare rooms for her father and sister the day they received the letter. There wasn't room for the others coming along, but they pulled out some large war tents and set them up like barracks for the guards. Two days had passed since they received the letter, and she only grew more eager by the day. She desperately wanted to see her sister again.

She and Samuel had spoken many times since their discussion in his study, and they planned on having dinner on Samuel's balcony again since it was supposed to be such a beautiful night. Darra arrived at his door just after dusk and knocked. He opened the door dressed in a set of fine clothes with a smile. She was excited about this dinner here with him. They shared their first kiss the last time she was in his room. She hoped they could rekindle what they had been developing that night. She looked stunning in a beige satin gown with a corseted top and pink embroidered flowers.

Samuel looked at her with soft eyes, and she blushed in response. They discussed their childhoods and upbringings in great detail throughout their meal, for which Darra was thankful. She felt it helped them both grow a lot closer in a short matter of time. Samuel walked to the balcony's edge when they finished eating and looked over the expansive hills leading to the woods. Then, he turned to her with a smile.

"How did I get so lucky with ye," he said in a hushed voice.

"I have nae idea," she responded with a laugh. She stood from her chair and walked to the balcony next to him. She rested her hands on the railing and admired the sprawling lands beyond her. He looked down at her hands and reached over to take them in his own. She turned and hugged him.

He wrapped his arms around her and held her in them tightly. They stood in their embrace before Darra slowly reached her hands towards his face and looked up at him. She smiled, stood on her tiptoes to meet his face, and pressed her lips against his. He tightened his grip around her and pulled her closer as they passionately kissed. Darra's hands slid from his face and down his neck as she softly ran them across his broad chest before draping them around his neck again. Samuel pulled away from her and leaned his forehead against hers with a smile. She giggled quietly and gently ran her finger over the top button of his tunic.

"What is it?" He asked softly, staring intensely into her bright green eyes.

"I think I'm ready," she replied after a moment with a coy smile. Samuel lit up and pulled away from her slightly.

"Ye're sure?" He said. Excitement rang in his voice as he watched her closely. She nodded her head and smiled in response. Samuel held his hand out for her to grab and led her from the balcony to his room, stopping as they reached his large bed.

He leaned down and held her face as he kissed her again, a long and passionate kiss. A fire burned between them as their hands fumbled across each other's bodies. Samuel lowered his mouth to kiss her neck. Darra let out a quiet moan as his lips grazed her soft skin, and she shivered as his tongue gently brushed against it. He pulled her closer and continued kissing her neck, as she seemed to enjoy it. Darra felt him growing against her while she moaned, his hands lowering on her body and slowly making their way to her behind.

She pulled away from him and slowly began untying the top of her dress. He watched her with a tender longing in his eyes. She could see his eagerness as she progressed more in undoing the ties. After she finished, she slowly dropped the dress to the ground around her and stepped out of it. She suddenly became timid, looking down and wrapping her arms around her slim waist.

Samuel slowly approached her and softly lifted her chin to look into her eyes. She shivered against the room's cold air and looked at him nervously. He leaned down and kissed her again, slow and tender. The nerves she had moments before disappeared as she wrapped her arms around his neck and passionately kissed him. Samuel leaned down to pick her up and carry her to the bed. He laid her down and stood beside the bed as he undressed. Darra stared at the ceiling in the room, her cheeks flushed with excitement and fear. She wasn't afraid of him at that moment, but she was scared of many other things. *Am I the first woman he's been with? What if I'm nae good at this? Will it hurt?* She thought as she waited for him to join her.

After a moment, he climbed on top of her and looked in her eyes, and she could see he seemed a bit nervous, too.

"Is this okay?" He asked her before he touched her. She nodded her head, and he lowered himself to her. He kissed her neck again before slowly working his way to her breasts. He softly ran his fingers across the peaks of her nipples and kissed the soft skin. Darra felt him between her legs, and her body tensed a bit. Samuel pulled away from her and looked up at her again.

"Are ye okay?" He asked in a calm tone.

"I'm just a bit nervous," she whispered in response.

"We donnae have to do this now. We can always wait-"

"I wannae," she said with certainty in her voice. He nodded and kissed her lips again. Darra quickly let the anxious thoughts float away, leaving her desire for Samuel again at the forefront of her mind. She ran her hands across his chest to feel his firm muscles before pulling him closer to her. She slowly pressed her hips closer to his member again.

A bell rang through the keep, and Samuel bolted to the window. He peaked to see about a dozen horses riding in the distance approaching the keep. He rushed to the side of the bed and quickly began putting his trousers and tunic back on.

"What is it?" Darra asked, pulling a blanket close to her chest to cover herself.

"They're here," he replied and turned to look at Darra. "I should be there to greet them," he said with an apologetic face. Then, he walked to the bed and kissed her once more before looking over himself in the mirror and leaving the room.

Darra sat in the bed for a moment, thinking about what had just happened. She was excited to see her family but wished they could have timed their visit better. Then, quickly, she sat up and dressed again, struggling to tie the ribbons by herself to look as if her chambermaids had helped her. After a few minutes, she walked to a mirror and fixed her hair before leaving to join her husband at the keep entrance.

~

Samuel rushed through the keep to reach the front gates before the Sloane clan. He grabbed Angus along the way, who was fully asleep when the bell rang, and they both waited outside as the horses rode in closer. He took a few deep breaths as he watched them approach. He was nervous for many reasons, the war resuming being the most important. He suddenly realized he could not see Shannon anywhere and whispered to Angus to have someone find her and keep her away from Laird Guthrie. Angus walked off for a moment and whispered to another guard. Samuel couldn't risk her running to Laird Guthrie and spreading lies to cause the clan harm.

After a few minutes, they finally approached with Laird Guthrie Sloane in the center. Behind sat a young girl strikingly similar to Darra in every way. Laird Sloane hopped off his horse first, followed by several of the guards accompanying him. His daughter was the last one off with the help of one of the other men.

Laird Sloane approached Samuel and Angus and surveilled them both before offering his hand. Samuel shook it firmly.

"Welcome, Laird Sloane. I hope your journey here was pleasant," Samuel said after pulling his hand away.

"Aye, it was, thank ye. I was expecting my daughter to be here to greet me too," he said with suspicion.

"She will be here shortly. We didnae expect ye all so late. She is just dressing now," Samuel responded. As if on cue, Darra walked through the front door of the keep in her beige gown. She paused when she saw her father standing before Samuel, then quickly rushed down the steps to greet him.

She threw her arms around her father's neck and kissed his cheek.

"Da! I've missed ye so much!" She exclaimed to him during their embrace. She looked over his shoulder and saw Deidre slowly walking up behind him. She let him go and made eye contact with her sister. They both ran into each other's arms and tightly hugged each other. Deidre started crying into Darra's shoulder as they hugged. "Ye've grown so much," she said as she held her younger sister at arm's length and looked her over.

"It's like looking in a mirror," her father said as he watched them with a wide smile. Then, he looked at Samuel with a more serious face. "We've got a lot to discuss." Samuel nodded his head and gestured for him to follow him inside.

"Angus, could ye take these fine men to the barracks," he said. Angus nodded his head and walked toward the guards. "We can talk in my study." Samuel walked inside of the keep, with Laird Sloane following close behind.

~

*D*arra was over the moon with excitement to see her sister again after what felt like years apart. She led her inside the keep to take her on a tour of her new home. Deidre asked about her arm, and she told her a slight lie. She said she just got lost in the woods, choosing not to mention her argument with Samuel.

"Who rode in with ye guys," Darra asked Deidre during their tour. She wanted to know if anyone she knew was here as well.

"I think the only one ye'd ken is Callum," Deidre responded halfheartedly as she looked over an old tapestry hanging on the wall.

Callum is here. Her stomach dropped as she thought about running into him on the grounds of the keep.

HIGHLAND INTRIGUE

*D*arra laid awake in bed most of the night. *Callum is here,* she thought continuously to herself. She once loved him with every fibre of her being, but she hadn't thought of him much since being here. *How much could I have loved him then?*

Callum was the first man she ever loved. She felt guilty as she remembered her giddy feelings when she saw him. She'd lay awake at night dreaming about him, praying someday he'd convince her father to allow them to wed. There was a time when her romantic adolescent dreams even seemed real to her. That's partly why she tried to convince her father not to marry her to Samuel. But he did, and those dreams dissipated, and new ones took their place, all involving Samuel.

She cared about Samuel more than she imagined she ever would. Even considering what she'd learned of him during the war, he was her husband, and she *loved* him. She never thought he'd be as gentle and caring as he was or as handsome. She spent hours debating if she should tell Samuel about Callum, but she wasn't sure how he'd react to the news.

Darra imagined if she told him, he might react poorly. They have yet to share their marriage bed, and it would be easy to kick her out and send her back to her old home with her father. She tried to picture him doing that but found it challenging. He wasn't hot-tempered. But he might be hurt by it; knowing she once kissed another man, and he wasn't her first might anger him in some ways. It was a delicate situation, and she decided the best plan was to avoid the subject altogether. She'd avoid Callum at all costs and pray the conversation never arose.

A knock sounded on her door just after she finally managed to fall asleep, and her chambermaids, Kailee and Kieren, walked in. Usually, they'd have a breakfast tray in their hands, but today they arrived empty-handed. Kailee walked to her wardrobe and pulled out an outfit for her to dress in.

"Laird Carrigan has requested breakfast in the dining hall, milady. Yer father and sister will be there as well." Kieren said as she softly roused Darra from her sleep.

Darra groggily dressed and followed them down the halls to join everyone for breakfast. However, she tried to compose herself along the way, as she thought it best not to let everyone worry about her by seeing her in distress.

"Pardon my saying so, Lady Carrigan, but ye seem," Kailee started to say before pausing, seemingly trying to find appropriate words, "ye seem a bit out of it all this morning. Is everything all right?"

"Thank ye, Kailee; I'll be fine. Just had a hard time falling asleep, is all," she replied with a half-smile. She felt the exhaustion in her limbs as they finally made their way to the hall, and she sat down in her chair at the head of the table.

Samuel's chair was empty. No doubt he planned to be the last one in the room. She was raised in a noble household, so she understood the importance of the formalities and the small mind games men would play to appear more powerful. She looked around the room and smiled when she noticed her father was missing too. Her husband would soon find out that showing off to her father would prove difficult. Laird Sloane wasn't much of a fighter, but he was a born leader and with that came cunning and wit most men couldn't keep up with.

After a few minutes, Samuel entered the room in elegant clothes; he wore a silky green tunic, finely tailored trousers, and wavy hair combed back. She thought he looked regal as he approached his seat beside her at the table. She could see the frustration in his eyes when he realized he'd come before her father. He looked around the room and saw Diedre sitting at the table with sleep heavy in her eyes.

"Good morning," he said in general to everyone in the room. "I trust ye found yer accommodations pleasant, Diedre?"

"Quite. Thank ye," Diedre said, perking up and smiling at Samuel. "Ye have a lovely home."

"I plan to give ye a full tour of it today," Darra said to her. Diedre smiled and opened her mouth the reply but was cut short by the entrance of their father.

"Ye didn't all have to wait for me to arrive," he said, walking towards the other end of the table and sitting across from Samuel.

"Laird Sloane, welcome and good morning," Samuel said. Darra noticed his posture straighten as he spoke. He nodded towards Arla, waiting by the door, and she rushed out of the room to bring food into the hall. They sat silently for a moment, all unsure of where the others' minds were. "I've rearranged my schedule so we'll have ample time to talk today," Samuel said to her father.

He nodded in response. Darra smiled to herself as she imagined how that meeting would go. She knew they would manage a way out of the situation that brought her father here, she hadn't written the letter, and if it came down to it, she would refuse to leave. But the image of her husband and father, both very powerful men in their own rights, having a contest of their wits to prove who might be more powerful was funny.

Arla brought food to the tables shortly after, and everyone in the room eagerly dined to distract from the overwhelming discomfort in the air. Darra looked at her husband and saw an uneasy look on his face and wished she could say something to comfort him, but she knew he wouldn't want her to acknowledge it. So instead, she laid her hand on his knee and softly squeezed it. He looked at her, and she flashed a comforting smile at him. She knew his meeting with her father today would be taxing, and she hoped the slight reassurance she was on his side might help him.

∾

*B*reakfast went over without any tense conversation, and for that, Samuel was thankful. But now, he would have to explain everything to Laird Sloane. He had tossed and turned all night long, trying to think of the best way to begin this conversation and what exactly he needed to tell him. He tried to think of all the possible questions Laird Sloane would ask him, trying to prepare answers. The decision of whether or not to tell him he was the one who killed his son, his heir, in combat weighed heavy on his mind. Should he decide to divulge his secret, Sloane might take it one of two ways: understanding they had been heated in battle and realize Samuel was protecting his land, or conversely, become so enraged as to retreat with Darra back to their clan, reigniting the war more heated than ever before.

Laird Sloane followed him down the halls to the study in silence. When they entered the room, Samuel sat at his place behind a large desk, and Laird Sloane sat down across from him. He watched his new father-in-law struggle and sigh as he bent his knees to sit.

"Laird Sloane," Samuel started to say...

"Call me Guthrie," he said in an exasperated tone, waving his hand to stop Samuel. "We're family now, after all." He let out a chuckle as he spoke.

"Indeed we are, and I thank ye for that. I've quite enjoyed my time so far with yer daughter," he paused to run through all of the scenarios one last time before they truly began talking. "I intend to answer any questions ye have. I want ye to know that I care for yer daughter, and I wouldn't do anything to harm her. I hope that I can prove that to ye."

"My daughter practically begged me nae to move forward with this marriage," Guthrie said stoically. "She tried to convince me it was all a ploy to ransom her off, that ye'd hold her hostage as if she'd be a toy to ye. Darra has always been dramatic, to say the least." Samuel smiled and nodded his head while Guthrie softly laughed. "After a while, she convinced me this was a mistake, but we both ken it was best for our clans." He leaned forward and rested his hands on the desk.

"She wants to make a difference here," Samuel replied. "Darra has seen how war has impacted our clans, and she wants to give life to these lands again. I admire her passion. Ye've done an excellent job raising her." He was sincere in everything he said; he thought so highly of Darra.

They'd only known each other for a short while, but he felt strongly about her - he loved her. The moment he laid eyes on her, he saw her passion and love for everything around her and her desire to change, and he so badly wanted to foster those tendencies. She was one of the most genuine and kind people he knew, and he felt lucky to be with her. Speaking to her father made him realize he needed to tell her how much he cared for her.

"I cannae take credit for that. My wife raised her," he paused and looked down at his hands for a moment. "Seeing her sitting next to ye, I could have sworn it was the ghost of my wife. She took all the best traits from her mother, and she learned well from her." He looked past Samuel through the window with a nostalgic smile. "What of ye and my daughter? Should I be expecting an heir soon?"

Samuel blushed and looked all over the room. He tried to think of the best way to answer the question, they were in the middle of attempting when he arrived, but that was only their first time together. While anticipating this question during the night, he planned on lying, but he knew that Laird Sloane would easily detect the lie.

"I havenae wanted to pressure her. As I said, I care for her. But I want her to be comfortable and feel like it's her decision, nae mine, nae yers," Guthrie nodded his head and sighed.

"I feared as much," Guthrie responded. "I'm glad ye're allowing her comfort and respect, but the peace treaty we made was contingent upon an heir." Samuel's heart dropped, and fear flooded his limbs. Now that Guthrie knew, he could end their marriage, and the war would restart. "I'm nae a young man, and I fear my bones wither daily. I donnae have much time left in this world. The Sloane Clan needs a leader," he said with a solemn face.

"What of yer other daughter?" Samuel asked a hint of desperation in his voice. He worried Guthrie would bring up the heir but knew there would likely be no way around it.

"She's young, too young for marriage. If I had a few years, I would have considered that, but I'm afraid I donnae have much longer," Guthrie said. Samuel looked him in the eyes and saw only exhaustion. He looked ill.

"What is going on to make ye think that?" he asked. Guthrie laughed heartily in response,

"When ye're my age, ye'll understand. Everyone's time must come eventually." He looked Samuel in the eyes as a seriousness fell over his face. "I might have a solution, though it may be temporary. Ye're brother, how old is he now?"

Darra was thrilled to spend time with her sister again. She hadn't been away from her for too long, but she missed so many things about her. How excited she'd get, the quiet snort when she laughed too hard, and afterward how embarrassed she'd be. She missed her clan, and having her sister here gave her a small piece of it. She found comfort in the Carrigan clan, but nothing compared to the home where she had been raised.

She walked Diedre all of the keep. She showed her the kitchens and introduced her to Arla (the sisters had been taken care of primarily by their maids and kitchen staff after their mother passed, so it was natural for them to respect them and treat them like family). Diedre complimented Arla for a beautiful breakfast, and the small woman blushed and smiled at her before she began preparing for their lunches. They walked arm in arm and admired the beautiful tapestries, old vases, paintings and many other decorations lining the walls and resting on tables throughout the keep. Darra was most excited to take her to the garden, though. Diedre loved nature and dreamt of exploring it just as Darra did, but their lands lacked woods, and the Sloane keep didn't have the beautifully tailored lawn with beds of flowers and fresh vegetables that they did here. She knew Diedre would be stunned by the blooming flowers and bright green grass surrounding them.

Even though she was enjoying her time with her sister, she was anxious about the conversations Samuel and her father were having. She prayed to herself that nothing would come of it, that her father would think all of this a misunderstanding and leave them be in the Carrigan Clan to start their family.

She was also worried she'd run into Callum. They constructed barracks on the grounds of the keep for Laird Sloane's entourage, and she hoped they wouldn't cross paths with him during their walk in the garden.

There was a small bustling outside as they made their way along the manicured grounds. She saw him in the distance. He stood outside the tents laughing with another man, both still in riding clothes. His eyes met hers briefly, and she looked away. Her heart skipped a beat, and she felt knots forming in her stomach. She quickened her step and rushed to the garden with Diedre.

She didn't want to speak to him. She couldn't. She spent all night thinking about how he must feel betrayed by her somehow. How hurt he might have been that she left, he knew it wasn't her choice, but they didn't leave on good terms. They fought the night before, and he abandoned her. Callum had planned to accompany her to the Carrigan keep, but he never showed up. She thought they were in love at one point, that he would whisk her away and marry her, but he abandoned her. She was happy with Samuel now, but before she met him, she was scared, and Callum had done nothing to help her.

She suddenly realized she was angry with him. She felt betrayed by him in some ways, and she felt guilty for that because she was happy with Samuel. She was now a married woman. She shouldn't harbour feelings for another man.

They sat down on the soft grass, and Diedre's face lit up. She inhaled the aroma of the blooming flowers and sighed with a bright smile. She looked around and admired all the bright colours highlighted under the cloudless blue sky.

"It is a beautiful home, Darra. Ye're so lucky," she said. A small smile grew on her face, and her cheeks reddened slightly.

"What is it?" Darra asked with a laugh.

"I just wasnae expecting Laird Carrigan to be as bonnie as he is," she said as she covered her face and started laughing. Darra shook her head and laughed with her.

"Between ye and me," she said before leaning in closer, "I didnae either."

"What is he like?" She asked, leaning on her elbows to bathe in the sun and listen to her sister.

"Surprisingly, he's kind and gentle, but also strong and very brave." She looked at her arm where the bandage from the wolf bite was. "He's nothing like I expected him to be, and that's a very good thing," she said, laughing.

"Do ye love him?" Diedre asked. Darra smiled and nodded her head. "That's so romantic! It's like something from a book, two lost souls arranged to marry and find themselves madly in love with each other." She paused for a moment and grabbed her sister's hand. "I'm very happy for ye, Darra. I ken how worried ye were." Darra squeezed her hand and nodded to her.

"Ye have to tell me everything that's been happening at home. I feel like I'm missing so much," Darra said.

"Nothing interesting has happened. Everyone sends regards, and a few people have moved away recently. Miranda is now betrothed," she said, listing off recent events.

"And who is Miranda marrying?" Darra interrupted with a hint of shock in her tone. She grew up with Miranda and found her to be cruel and mean. Miranda always coveted others for things they had and quickly spread rumours around to make others look bad. She wanted to give everyone the benefit of the doubt and see good, but Miranda made it hard.

"Callum," Diedre said. "He started courting her shortly after ye left. Apparently, they're in love." She shrugged as if she could read Darra's mind and agreed with her sister's thoughts.

"That's a pairing I never thought I'd see," Darra said after a moment. She gritted her teeth at the thought of them together. *Am I jealous,* she thought, realizing how annoyed she was at hearing the news.

They walked back to the keep in time for lunch, Darra asked Arla to bring their lunches to her room, and she did. They sat in chairs by the window and enjoyed their lunches together.

"When are ye set to leave?" Darra asked.

"In a few days, I believe," Deidre answered, a fox-like smile playing at her lips. "Are ye that eager to be rid of us?"

"Not at all! I'm planning a festival for the clan, something to thank them for welcoming me and coming to my aid in the woods. I'm so happy ye will both be here for it!"

"That sounds lovely. I'd be happy to help prepare for it. Ye ken I've got quite the knack for decorating," Diedre smiled.

"Well, I was supposed to work on it today, and yer distraction has kept me from my duties," Darra said jokingly. "I could certainly use all the help I can get."

They finished their lunches and talked for the remainder of the afternoon until Kailee interrupted them for dinner.

Guthrie handed Samuel a folded piece of paper, wrinkled and ripped from being read many times and carried in his pockets. Samuel glanced over the paper and immediately recognized it as what must be the letter he received that made him come all this way to confront him.

> Dear Father,
>
> My marriage to Laird Carrigan was a mistake. He is a brute of a man. I am writing to you with a broken arm and a head injury. I fear for my life in this clan. I am writing for guidance. I need to stay - for peace - but I don't know how to go on like this.
> Sending my love,
> Darra

Samuel sighed as he read the note. He immediately recognized it was not Darra's handwriting. They had exchanged messages in the past, and her delicate hand was poorly forged on this paper. So when he first heard Laird Sloane had received a letter, he knew it must have been from Shannon. She'd stop at nothing to make his life miserable.

He pulled open one of the drawers on his desk, where he knew he placed the first letter she'd written him asking him to accompany her to dinner. He fished around in it for a moment before realizing it was missing. *Shannon!* he thought as he shut the drawer and looked back at Guthrie. Had she broken into his study and stolen the letter?

"I had another letter from Darra that seems to be missing now. I thought we might compare the two of them," he said annoyedly. "This looks like a forgery to me. But if you need to be certain, we can always have Darra write something and compare-"

"That willnae be necessary. I've seen my daughter's handwriting countless times. I thought it just might be a forgery." He laughed again. Samuel couldn't help but feel a bit frustrated with him. If he thought it might be a forgery, why would he visit under the pretense that he believed it to be real? Samuel had been anxiously awaiting his arrival and needlessly worrying about the war resuming because of this letter.

"Might I ask, if ye ken it f a forgery, why come all this way?" he asked, trying to hide the annoyance in his voice.

"I wanted to see my daughter one last time," he said quietly. Samuel felt suddenly guilty for questioning him.

"Do either of yer daughters ken you feel your time is coming?" he asked quietly.

"Nae, not yet. I plan to tell both of them before I leave for my lands. So please do me a favour and donnae mention this to Darra yet," he said. Samuel nodded at him.

They finished their business in the afternoon, just after lunchtime. Samuel walked through the halls looking for Angus. He was his most trusted advisor and could advise on everything they had just discussed.

Laird Sloane wanted to take his brother, Duncan, in as a ward. He planned to train him to lead the clan when he passed away.

Samuel couldn't decide whether he thought it was a good idea. At first, it seems an obvious decision to ensure the clan has a leader since there is no other heir to rule. But the more he thought about it, the more dangerous the proposal seemed; if Duncan led the Sloane clan, Shannon would likely be in his ear. She had proven more cunning than he would have given her credit for, and he couldn't risk her having any power. Moreover, she despised him so much that he had no doubt she would instigate war at the first opportunity to make him suffer.

Samuel found Angus walking through the halls with the group of men that travelled here with Laird Sloane. Angus was giving them all a detailed tour of the keep, one of his favourite things to do for guests. Angus was keenly interested in the various heirlooms and knew the history of most items in the keep, like a Carrigan family historian.

"Why donnae ye all look at some tapestries here in the great hall? I should only be a moment with our Laird," Angus said as Samuel walked up to him and asked him to accompany him to his balcony for a discussion. "Do ye think it's wise to leave them all unattended?" He wondered aloud when they were out of earshot.

"I donnae think they mean any harm," he said as they walked towards his room. They entered and walked out onto Samuel's balcony and sat down. "I just finished my conversation with Laird Sloane. He wants to take Duncan as a ward because we've yet to produce an heir. He fears he'll die soon and wants to make sure there's a familial heir."

"That sounds too good to be true. That would have Carrigans leading both clans," Angus said with a slight chin scratch as he ran the scenario over in his mind.

"My concern is Shannon. She cannae be anywhere near him if he's in power. And he's just a child, Angus. He cannae lead an entire clan by himself," Samuel said, his voice strained from exhaustion.

"Shannon in his ear would not bode well for us," he shook his head. "But what are we to do about it? If we say nae, what might happen?" He paused for a moment to think about the possibilities.

"Where is Shannon?" He had asked Angus to get rid of her while the Sloane entourage was there. He was sure she'd sent the letter then and needed to be sure she wouldn't interfere with anything else.

"She's in town with two of the guards," Angus answered. "They were instructed to keep an eye on her and detain her in a cabin there. It's comfortable. She's probably enjoying the quiet time alone."

Samuel's face lit up as if a brilliant idea crossed his mind. It was an idea that would solve their problems, but it wasn't kind, and he couldn't anticipate how Shannon would react.

"What if we send the boy away while Shannon is gone," he said in a hushed tone. "We willnae have to deal with her threats, and she willnae even ken where he is."

"Take a child away from his mother?" Angus asked rhetorically. "That's beyond cruel, Samuel. I dislike the woman as much as ye, but I couldnae do that."

"I donnae want to, but it might be the only option. Shannon will never allow us to send him without her, and it is too high of a risk to let her accompany him" he replied in a defensive tone. "Unless we can think of anything else, it might be the only option."

"What of Darra's relatives?" He asked in a pleading tone. "She must have someone else who can take over the role."

"If I ask Darra, she'll be suspicious of why her father needs someone now," Samuel replied, "he asked me not to mention his condition to her. He wants to tell her himself. So, unfortunately, we must decide without her input." Angus sighed and pinched the center of his forehead in frustration.

"I see nae other option," he paused and looked Samuel in his eyes, "but if that is what it comes down to, I will have nae part in it." Angus stood and left the room.

Samuel shook his head, frustrated with the entire situation. He understood why Angus was so upset about it. Breaking apart a family is not an easy task by any means, and it was sure to weigh heavy on the conscience of those involved.

Dinner was much more pleasant than breakfast. Darra couldn't wait to talk to Samuel and find out precisely what happened during his meeting with her father. Both men seemed to be in good spirits. They were joined at the table by her father, Diedre, Angus, and Duncan. Darra watched warmly as her father interacted with Samuel's young half-brother. He was always good with children. She fondly remembered times he'd play games with her as a child and the stories he'd tell her. The dramatic flare he often told her she had likely came from those tales of gallant heroes he would tell.

But watching him with Duncan only reminded her of how he was with her brother - his son - and how he changed when he learned he had been killed in battle. The wounds reopened within her, and she was pained knowing her husband had killed him. Her father had no idea he was sitting in the same room as him. She decided long before they arrived that she would not tell him. It would be too great a risk if he were to be angry. The war resuming was the last thing she wanted, and it was a small price to pay to keep the people of her clan safe.

They all ate their meals peacefully, sharing a few stories of their pasts. Laughter filled the dining hall, and Darra was happy about it.

"I need to speak to ye after supper," Samuel whispered to Darra during the meal's commotion. She nodded her head and smiled. She didn't sense anything to worry about in his tone, but she couldn't help but let her mind wander.

After the meal, she followed him back to his chambers, eager to find out what he had to say. When they were finally alone, he sat on the edge of his bed and rubbed his temples. Her heart dropped, thinking there was something terribly wrong.

"What's the matter?" She asked and rushed to sit beside him on the bed.

"I'm just a bit stressed, and I didnae sleep last night," he replied. He stared at her for a moment and smiled. He loved that she cared about him. After everything Samuel had done in his life, she cared about him. He was lucky to have her. He wanted to tell her how he felt. How he cared so much and *loved* her, but the words couldn't make their way to his lips. He wanted to tell her at the perfect moment. She deserved no less than that.

"How was your talk with my father?" she asked him eagerly.

"Aye, it turns out he suspected it was a forgery the whole time," he replied with a small laugh. Darra rolled her eyes and scoffed.

"He always tells me I'm dramatic," she laughed and shook her head.

Samuel went over almost everything from their conversation, leaving out all the details of Guthrie, fearing his death soon.

"Are ye sure sending Duncan is the right idea? We did want to try for an heir just yesterday; perhaps it isnae as far off as we thought," she said with blush high on her cheeks. Samuel smiled at her and laughed softly.

"Sadly, I didnae tell yer father his arrival last night interrupted our first ... attempt. Perhaps that might have given me some bargaining leverage."

She laughed and looked into his eyes with a smile. Samuel watched her gaze drop to his lips, then his neck, and linger on the top button of his tunic. He longed for her; the intensity of the night before was still strong. He had longed for her since the moment he laid eyes on her riding down the trail on her horse, and just last night, she laid naked in his bed, ready to give herself over to him and start a family. Only today did he realize how deeply he felt for her and wanted to show that.

He reached his hand to her face and pulled it towards his. He kissed her lips, soft at first, but he grew hungry with desire as every second passed. He slid his tongue inside her mouth and savoured her taste and the soft moans that escaped her throat. He pulled away from her for a moment to breathe, and she quickly pulled him back to kiss more. He lowered his mouth and kissed her neck, and she shuddered as he did. Her pleasure excites him, and he lays her down on the bed. She smiled at him and rubbed her hands against the fabric of his tunic, feeling his broad shoulders.

"Make love to me," she moaned into his ear as he kissed the nape of her neck.

He slowly began untying the front of her corset to undress her, and she unbuttoned his tunic. When she finished, she rubbed his chest. He looked down to see her eyes full of passion and desire as she looked at him. When he finished untying her corset, he pulled the chemise she wore over her head. He admired her body for a moment, her fingers toying with the button of his trousers. Her fingers softly brushed against his aroused member through the fabric. Each seemingly accidental caress increased his desire.

She unbuttoned his pants and pulled them down with reddened cheeks. He lowered himself onto her again and kissed the skin between her breasts. He cupped one and toyed with her peaked nipple before taking it into his mouth. She ran her fingers through his hair and moaned as his tongue teased her. He kissed her lips again and gently pressed himself against her. She gasped softly and bit her lips when she felt how aroused he was with her.

Darra wrapped her legs around his waist and pulled him close to her. He looked her in the eyes to confirm everything was alright, and she nodded, eager to take him inside her. He gently pushed his way inside her, ensuring she was comfortable the whole time. He sighed and tried to control himself as he thrust slowly; he wanted to make this as pleasurable for her as possible. He pressed his mouth against hers, both moaning softly as they made love. Soon after, her moans quickened and grew louder, he felt her body shudder beneath him, and he quickened his pace. Finally, she started crying out in pleasure, and he lost control of hearing it. He thrust deep within her and slowed his pace with a deep guttural moan as he finished inside her.

Darra woke at sunrise in Samuel's arms. She saw his eyes groggily opening as he squeezed her tightly against himself. He kissed her forehead and brushed her hair behind her ear. She savoured every second before she had to leave to begin her day. She wished she could stay there forever, but the festival was the next day, and she needed to catch up on preparations.

"Donnae go," Samuel whispered between soft kisses as she tried to leave his bed.

"I have to," she whispered back. "Diedre and my chambermaids should already be in the great hall preparing." He groaned as she left his bed and dressed to leave. She kissed him goodbye one last time and left the room.

She tiptoed through the halls to avoid drawing attention to herself. Samuel was her husband, but this was the first time they'd made love. She wasn't sure how to handle this part of their relationship yet. Unfortunately, she'd need to walk past the great hall to get to her room.

As soon as the three girls saw her walk down the hall in the clothes she'd worn the night before, huge smiles crossed their faces. She knew they would all want to ask them questions about her night, and she needed to detour the conversation before they could.

"Good morning. I'm glad ye're all here. I'm gonnae go change and take a quick bath, and I'll continue preparing after," Darra said, brushing past them all without explaining anything. She could feel them watching her walk away.

"Do you want one of us to draw yer bath?" Kailee asked her.

"It would be a better help to continue this, for now, thank ye," she quickly replied as she walked through the hall towards her chamber. "That wisnae so bad," she whispered to herself.

Her breath caught in her throat as she opened the door to her room. Sitting casually on her bed was Callum. He jumped up as soon as she entered and bowed to her. She quickly rushed in and closed the door tightly behind her.

"What are ye doing here?" She said in a hushed yell.

"I've been waiting for ye here all night," he said in a hushed tone as he slowly approached her. She stared at him in shock, utterly unsure of what to do. "I was worried when Laird Sloane received the letter indicating ye were hurt." Callum stood in front of her and gently grabbed her injured arm. She winced when he rested a hand on the bandages from the bite. "He'll pay for what he's done to ye."

"What?" She managed to say, her mind was racing with questions, yet she couldn't vocalize any of them.

"I shouldnae have let this happen. Ye asked me to save ye, and I didnae. And now my love is in danger." She opened her mouth to speak, but no words escaped her lips. Before she could attempt again, Callum's hands gripped her waist, and he pulled her close to him and kissed her. His grip was too tight for her to slip away quickly, but she pushed him and backed away.

"What are ye doing?" she exclaimed. "I'm married now, and I'm happy here. Samuell has done nothing to harm me. So how did ye even get in here?"

"I veered off on a tour of the keep yesterday when yer husband pulled Angus aside to talk, I was waiting for ye last night, but ye never showed."

"I was with my *husband*," Darra replied sternly. "Explain *why* ye are here right now, or I will scream, and every guard in this keep will drag ye out of here."

"This is what ye wanted, Darra." He paused for a moment and looked around the room. "Are all the feelings ye had for me gone? Were they ever really there?" he said, his voice slightly raised. Darra gestured for him to lower his voice again.

"I *loved* ye, Callum," she said in a hushed tone, "everything I said was true; all of the feelings *were* true. But things are different now."

"Those feelings donnae just disappear. I've loved ye all my life," he said in a desperate tone. "I'm doing what ye asked me to do. I came here to *save* ye, Darra."

There was a time when she would have been enamoured with the idea of being rescued. She would have seen this as a grand romantic gesture and swooned into Callum's arms. That seemed ages ago, but it wasn't that long. Before leaving her home, she had asked Callum to run away with her. She had meant it in those moments and thought she loved him. Things were different then, and now she was in love with Samuel.

"Callum," she said softly, reaching for his hand, "that was before I was here. I cannae go back now."

"We willnae be going back. I've made arrangements with a new clan; we'll start fresh there," he moved closer and grabbed her hands. "There's a farm we can live on, it will be a simple life, but we'll have each other. We can finally be together."

"That wasnae possible then, and it isnae now." She pulled away and walked to the chair by the window, motioning for him to sit across from her. He walked over and sat down, staring at her longingly.

"Darra," he whispered, "ye donnae need to be afraid. I'll protect ye. Ye're safe with me. Ye always have been." She could see the lust in his eyes and sense something else. A possessiveness that had always been there, just below the surface.

"Aye, where were ye the day I left then?" She couldn't stop herself from asking the question. It had been on her mind since he arrived and hearing him talk like this reminded her of the hurt she felt when he didn't ride with her to say goodbye. "Ye were supposed to come here with me, and ye didnae show up." He stood from his chair and paced in the room for a moment. Then, walking over to a water pitcher sitting on her end table, he poured two glasses. He handed her a drink and sat back down as he took a sip.

"I couldnae bear just handing ye over to Samuel The Cruel Carrigan. There was nothing I could do then," he said quietly. "I've loved ye since we were young. We've planned our lives together for years. That must count for something?" She took a long sip of her drink and set the glass down on the small table by them.

"I'm sorry, Callum, but I am happy here," she said sternly. "There isnae anything you can do about it now." He stared at her for a moment with a blank face.

"Isnae?" he asked. Darra constricted her face in confusion as he asked that. Then, slowly, she shook her head, and just as she did, she realized the room around her was spinning.

"Ye need to leave," she said quickly and stood to walk to the door. She stopped halfway through to steady herself on her footboard, then continued to the door. She lost her footing as she reached for the knob and fell to the ground. She groaned as her injured arm clashed with the cold stone floor. She looked up to see Callum kneeling to her. He brushed the hair from her face in a blur. Each time she blinked, she faded from the world more. She tried to force her eyes open, but they, too, collapsed.

Samuel thought about the night before with a giant smile on his face. He and Darra finally made love, and he was thrilled about it. Their relationship now seemed genuine. They had both been through so much in their lives but had somehow managed to come together, and everything seemed perfect. Just that morning, he held her in his arms and prayed he could wake next to her every morning for the rest of his life, and he would do anything to ensure he could.

He dressed and began going about his day. With Laird Sloane's sudden arrival, Samuel had put some of his other duties aside to address more pressing concerns. He had dozens of letters and documents to pour over for the people of his clan, minor land disputes, marriage licenses, taxation agreements, and general grievances within the town. His father would have left Angus to take care of these things and instead would have trained his fighters or spent days bonding with them in town at the small tavern. Samuel remembered when he was a boy training with his father, how strong he was, and how the people in the town admired him for his physical strength over all else. He did too, but he knew there was more to leading than being strong. When his father died, and Samuel had become the new Laird, Samuel asked Angus to show him all of his duties. He thought it just as essential to be sharp in mind. He often wondered if the war might have ended sooner if his father also had.

Angus met him in his study with more papers for them to sign. Samuel asked him for his help to catch up after Laird Sloane's arrival. He skipped breakfast that morning and got right to work. By the time Arla knocked on the study door and brought them fresh tea and a light lunch, they'd managed to get halfway through the pile, primarily thanks to Angus. Samuel had been working at a slow pace all morning. His mind was elsewhere, and he was very distracted thinking about Darra.

"Is everything alright?" Angus asked him between large spoonfuls of soup.

"Aye. For the first time in a while, I feel everything is fine." He smiled at his advisor and started reading over more papers to busy himself and avoid more questions. He thought for a while and realized he hadn't felt this content in years and couldn't help but worry if it was just the calm before the storm. Things had a history of falling apart for him when he let down his guard.

He took a break from his duties near the end of the day to find his wife. He wanted to see how the festival preparations were going and lend a hand to alleviate her stress. The earlier she finished, the better, as he hoped they might be able to spend the night together again.

Diedre and Darra's chambermaids were in the great hall assembling floral arrangements when he walked in. The three of them laughed and talked happily while they worked.

"Pardon me, ladies, but have any of ye seen my wife lately?" He asked in a calm tone. The three of them stopped laughing and looked up at him. He could see faint smiles forming on their lips and blush on their cheeks. *Darra must have told them everything about last night,* he thought to himself with a soft smile. The thought of Darra sitting with them and giving them every detail and the three of them gushing over it all made him laugh a bit.

"I havenae seen her since this morning," Diedre said, "she was going to her chamber. She said she would bathe and continue working the festival preparations."

"And she wasnae with the three of you for that?" he asked a slight alarm in his voice. He figured it would be here or the garden if she were anywhere. The three girls shook their heads no and looked toward each other. He thanked them and left the room. He walked outside towards the garden and began looking for her.

The garden was full of people; there were landscapers trimming hedges, people setting up long tables, and numerous people running around carrying equipment and items to and from the keep. He looked through the people for Darra and couldn't find her. He walked around the grounds hoping he'd see her hanging a banner or picking flowers.

Perhaps she needed to go into town, he thought as he made his way to the stables. Before asking the attendant there if he'd seen his wife, he realized all his horses were present and accounted. The only other horses there were those of the riders who came in with Laird Sloane. He walked back to the keep and began searching for her inside. He went first to the dining hall. It was close to supper time, but he did not find her there. He walked to the kitchens. If anyone might know where she'd gotten off to, it could be Arla. She seemed to know about all the goings-on of the keep.

"Arla, have ye seen Darra?" He asked as soon as he walked in. He couldn't control the worry in his voice when he spoke to her. Arla stood on a chair by the stove, mixing something in a pot nearly as large as she was. She stepped down and shook her head no.

"Nae, I havenae seen her today, I'm afraid. Have ye checked with Kailee and Kieren? They mentioned they'd be with her today planning for the festival," she replied in a calming tone. He nodded his head and turned to walk away.

"If ye see her, please let me know," he said before walking away. He rushed down the halls to her room to see if she was there. He said a silent prayer along the way that he'd find her at a table reading over her plans, checking items off a list to ensure a smooth day tomorrow. *That must be where she is; she has to be,* he thought as he approached her door. He knocked softly, and when there was no response, he pushed the door open and found an empty room. He walked in and stood for a moment, unsure where to go from there. *Where could she be?* He thought desperately.

How could this happen to him again? He just got her back after she ran off into the woods, and she was so injured. The idea of her being lost and afraid somewhere worried him.

He left her room and looked all over the keep for her, searching every room. He was careful not to raise any alarms while he did so. The last thing he needed was Laird Sloane thinking she was unsafe here. When he didn't find her, he went to see Angus so that he could assemble a search party for her. Angus left to gather some of their best men to begin looking all over town for her as soon as Samuel told him she was missing.

The last thing Samuel needed to do was speak to Laird Sloane. His mind raced as he walked through the halls to find his father-in-law. He found him in a small parlour resting in a chair and staring out the window. Samuel watched him for a moment before approaching, his breaths deep and heavy as if something were constructing him. *What if this is his doing,* he thought. Samuel tried to force his worries away, but the previous day's conversation with Laird Sloane reminded him how much Darra's father *needed* an heir. What if he took his daughter away and planned to remarry her to someone else? It quickly started to consume his mind. It was the only logical explanation to him. Darra would not leave him on her own, she cared about him deeply, and he knew that. Just this morning, they shared tender kisses, and everything was perfect. There is no way she'd willingly leave.

"Have ye seen Darra?" asked Samuel. The old Laird turned slowly to face Samuel. He looked at him with confusion and shook his head. "I cannae find her anywhere. No one has seen her since this morning." Laird Sloane stood from his chair and walked towards him, he moved as quickly as he could, but his old bones slowed him.

"Are there people looking for her?" He asked nervously.

"Angus is assembling a search party now," he replied. He looked at the worry in his withered face and realized he was foolish to think it was him.

Just after Samuel said his name, Angus burst through the door out of breath and stopped when he saw Laird Sloane.

"What is the news?" Samuel eagerly asked him.

"I asked some men to search the grounds, and they found something," he said gravely. Samuel's heart sank, fearing the worst. "In her window, a long rope leads to the ground with tracks leading away."

"So, we'll follow the tracks and find her then," Laird Sloane said quickly.

"That's not all," Angus interrupted. "One of yer men is missing too."

Trees waved high in the air, and the sound of their whispers soothed the headache with which Darra awoke. Her vision was still blurry, and she tried to blink it away. As she did, she found herself fading once again into darkness.

She went on like that for what felt like days, but in reality, it was mere hours. She savoured her dreams while she was asleep. The brief escape from her waking nightmare was welcome.

She dreamt of her childhood mostly. The days she spent with her mother; she was a shadow to her, always following her and replicating everything she did. She missed her more than anything and wished that she were still around to teach Diedre all the things she did for her. In one of her dreams, her mother was still alive and leading the clan herself. The people in the clan didn't seem to mind either, the war was over and a kind, just leader saw to their affairs. The pride she felt in her dream carried her through hours of her real-life travel.

Once again, she woke. Each time her eyes opened, the world came more into focus. This time she could make out Callum sitting behind her on his horse with the reins in his hand. Her hands were tied in front of her, and a small rope was tied around her waist. She realized that was to hold her upright against Callum.

"Where am I?" she slurred groggily, her voice hoarse as she finally spoke.

"We're about a day's ride from our new lives, my love," he replied softly.

"Samuel..." she said quietly and drifted off again.

~

Samuel followed Angus to the keep grounds. He found a knotted rope hanging from Darra's window and horse tracks leading away.

"She was taken," he said gravely, assessing the situation.

"Which of my men is missing?" Laird Sloane asked.

"The other men said they havenae seen Callum since yesterday," Angus replied.

Diedre rushed towards them with a panicked look on her face. "Is it true?" She asked breathlessly. "She's missing?" Her father nodded his head and wrapped an arm around her while she cried into him.

"I'm gonnae find her, donnae ye worry," Samuel said before he stormed off. He rushed through the castle to grab his sword and prepare to leave. He had tracked her down before; he could do it again. And he was going to make sure whoever this Callum was would pay.

As Samuel prepared to leave, Laird Sloane rushed into the stables with a longbow in hand.

"I'm coming with ye," he said and nodded to the stable boy to prepare his horse for him.

"It may be a long journey. Are ye certain ye're up for it?" Samuel asked. He understood the need for him to come along, his daughter abducted by one of his men, but he was worried his age and condition would slow him. Samuel couldn't afford to waste time right now.

"I may be old, but I always have been a keen tracker. She's my daughter, and he's from my clan. So, I should be the one to see to his punishment," he said with a nod. It was final. He would come along.

His horse was promptly ready, and they took off to follow the tracks to the woods. Both men kept their eyes to the ground to follow them without error. Samuel planned to track them until he eventually caught up with them, he would push himself and his horse to the limit to catch up to them as they rested overnight, but now with Laird Sloane here, they would have to stop and rest. He worried it would put him further behind than he'd like.

The sunset in the sky and following the tracks grew harder each second. Samuel kept a close eye on Laird Sloane to ensure he was still okay with the journey. Finally, they stopped briefly after some time to let their horses drink from a small stream. Samuel leaned against a tall tree waiting for them, watching Laird Sloane slowly sit down on a fallen log with a pained groan.

"I havenae ridden like that in some time," he said once he was as comfortable as he could be on the log.

"I'm worried ye'll hurt yourself if ye go any further," he replied thoughtfully. "The terrain could worsen, and we'll have to move through the night to catch up with them. The possibility of an accident is too high for ye." Laird Sloane sighed and nodded his head.

"I donnae ken what I was thinking by coming anyway," he softly said aloud, although primarily to himself. Samuel didn't want to push him further, to spare his pride.

"This Callum man, what do you ken of him?" He asked to change the subject.

"He was one of my most trusted guards. I've been working with him for years since he was a wee boy," he said in a confused tone. "His father was my chieftain for years. But unfortunately, the father died in battle. Callum vowed to avenge his father's death against yer clan." He paused for a moment and sighed. "Perhaps this is his way of doing so now that the war is over."

"Why would he take Darra away," he thought aloud, "there must be something more to all of this."

"He and Darra were close. They grew up together. I don't ken how he could harm her," he said.

"Is it possible he loved her?" Samuel said through gritted teeth.

"It could be," he said slowly, "I donnae think she would reciprocate, though. She is always kind to everyone. I could see how he might misinterpret that kindness. But he's marrying another lass soon."

"That's never stopped a man before," he said in an exhausted voice. He stepped away from his tree, walked to the horses, and pulled them away from the stream. He then readied himself to hop on his steed. "Ye should head back to the keep and rest. I'll bring her back safely, and I can promise ye that." Laird Sloane nodded his head and looked to the ground. Samuel felt terrible that he made the older man feel weak, a man's pride was integral, and he had disregarded that. But his safety and well-being would be of utmost importance to Darra, and he had to ensure that more than anything.

Samuel hopped on his horse's back and turned it to begin following the tracks again. Before he was entirely out of earshot, he heard Laird Sloane calling for him. He stopped and turned around. Guthrie presented the longbow for him to take. Samuel took it in his hands, he wasn't much of a marksman, but he could handle any weapon relatively well - that's how he had been bestowed with the Carrigan the Cruel moniker, after all.

"This bow has been passed through many generations of the Sloane family," Guthrie said, "It seems right ye have it and pass it on to yer children." Samuel nodded at him and strapped the bow and quiver to his back before turning away again.

With that, he set off into the night, following tracks in the woods to find his wife. He would bring her home safely, and anyone seeing her harmed would regret it.

SAVED BY THE HIGHLANDER

The world came fully into focus around dusk. Darra didn't know how long it had been since they had left the keep. Her mind was a blur as she dozed in and out of consciousness on horseback. She would momentarily forget her predicament before seeing her hands tied in front of her. She remembered waking up in a haze several times as they rode past lush trees and puffy white clouds high in the sky.

She had hoped this was all just a dream, that she was still next to Samuel with his arms wrapped around her. *He'll find me. He has to,* she thought. She spent a while trying to find a way to escape her captor. Though she felt like she could wiggle out of the ropes that bound her hands, Darra didn't think she could outrun Callum. *Perhaps I say I need to relieve myself. Surely he'd give me a moment's privacy for that, and I could escape.* But then she remembered Callum was an excellent tracker; he had been one of her father's best hunters.

It was clear that Samuel was her only hope and she despised feeling helpless. She was a strong, intelligent woman and could be self-reliant, but Samuel would now come to her rescue twice because of situations in which she'd found herself. *I should have walked out of that room the minute I saw him.* She regretted even giving him the chance to explain himself to her, part of her thought they might owe it to one another to have a conversation, but when he kissed her, she should have ended it.

She tried to push those thoughts away. There was no sense in focusing on past mistakes when she needed to focus on how to escape now.

"Will we be stopping to rest soon?" she asked Callum, trying to hide the disdain in her tone.

"Aye. We'll be stopping shortly, my love," he replied quickly.

Maybe Samuel can catch up to us during our rest, she hoped silently. She took comfort in knowing that if Samuel were indeed searching for her, he wouldn't rest until he was successful.

~

As the sun set, the tracks Callum had left behind grew harder to follow. Samuel strained his eyes atop his horse to follow them in the dirt, becoming increasingly worried for his wife's safety every moment. He didn't know why this man had taken her. Did he wish her harm? Was this a ransom attempt? His mind raced as he worked through the reasons this could have happened. One thought crossed his mind that he quickly tried to shove aside, but it crept back in. *Did she want to go with him?*

It was a challenging idea to take in, but it could explain why there were no signs of any struggle. Indeed, Darra would have fought if taken from the keep against her will, so not seeing such signs allowed this new fear to creep up on Samuel. *Either way, when I find her, I'll have my answers,* he thought to try and comfort himself.

As he continued through the woods, he thought of all the different scenarios and how he would react to ensure Darra was safe. He knew Laird Sloane would want this man alive so he could see to his punishment as he was one of his own. But Samuel feared he would struggle to maintain his composure when they met. He wanted to ensure he respected his new father-in-law's wishes, but Darra was his wife now, and Samuel felt he deserved a say in what happened to Callum.

He let his anger fuel him as he rode on through the night, steadfast in his journey to rescue his new bride. The tracks were difficult to follow as the sun fully set, but he didn't let that hinder him. Instead, when the tracks were hard to follow on horseback, he hopped off and followed on foot to get a closer look. He was determined to find her as soon as possible and hoped he could catch up quickly. *Perhaps I can catch them resting,* he thought. If they camp for the night, he would indeed catch up and could catch Callum off guard. He didn't know much of Callum's skills firsthand, but Laird Sloane had told him he was a good hunter and ranked highly within the Sloane clan.

Samuel wondered if they had faced each other in battle; if they had, Callum would most certainly know of Carrigan the Cruel. This Callum must either be very brave or very foolish, he thought. Any man who would challenge Samuel this way was either a great fool or arrogant enough to consider the challenge would be a fair fight. For the first time in his life, Samuel welcomed the battle that awaited him.

∽

Not long after the sun set completely, they stopped for the night. Darra was thankful for the break for many reasons, mainly to rest her sore muscles. She had never ridden a horse for so long, every gallop sending aches of pain through her body, exacerbated by the ropes around her wrists and waist preventing her from finding a more comfortable position.

Callum hopped down from the horse and helped Darra to her feet. She winced as she was pulled down the horse's side and placed on her feet. She jerked her arms away from him when she was on her feet, and he responded with a quiet scoff before grabbing her arm and walking her to a small clearing in the woods.

"Have a seat," Callum said, pointing to a fallen log. Darra sat down and rested her hands on her lap. She took a deep breath and looked around her for an escape route. She sighed when she realized it was too dark to get a good look at her surroundings.

Perhaps I should wait until dawn and sneak away, she thought. *But what of these damned ties on my wrists?* She became increasingly hopeless as she considered the various ways back to the keep. Even if she did escape Callum, she was asleep for most of her journey here and likely wouldn't be able to find her way back. She had no experience with anything related to survival in the woodlands. She was familiar with some different herbs and flowers from things she'd read in books, but she'd be lost as far as hunting, foraging, or tracking to find her way back to the keep. She had two options: wait for Samuel to find her or stay with Callum and hope she could convince him to bring her back.

She watched silently as Callum gathered small sticks and twigs for kindling to start a fire. Then, assessing the situation, she realized her best chance of ensuring her safety and eventual release was to appeal to Callum.

"Callum," she said softly, waiting for him to look up at her and acknowledge her before speaking more. "Have you thought about what ye'll do if Samuel or my father find us?"

She made sure to keep her voice light and calm to keep from upsetting him.

"I have," he responded in a resolute voice. "I'm nae sure you'd be happy with my plans, Darra."

"What do you mean?" She asked, her tone raising slightly from a wave of worry that overtook her.

"I willnae let them take you willingly," he said in a low voice before focusing on his fire. Darra's blood ran cold as she realized what he meant. He would fight for her and risk his own life for his pride - or he might kill whoever was on their way to rescue her.

"It doesnnae need to be this way, Callum. We can turn back now, and I'll tell them someone else took me. That ye saw them and chased them, and that ye *rescued* me. Ye'll be a hero, Callum," she pleaded with him.

"Ye wanted this, ye begged me to save ye, and that's what I'm doing now," he replied in a frustrated tone. "Ye must nae ken to whom ye're married! He's a cruel beast. Tell me, has he told ye of his battlefield conquests? His reputation as Carrigan the Cruel was well earned."

"He had to fight, just as you did!" Darra quickly replied in a defensive voice.

"I fought to defend my clan and the lives of all the helpless souls within it. He fought for blood. He relished in slaying yer people. Ye're nae safe with him, Darra." His tone was final. He wanted to end the conversation there, but Darra would not let him slander her husband that way.

"He's told me everything, how he wished and prayed it could have been any other way, and carries the souls of every slain man upon his shoulders," She paused for a moment and glared at Callum. "He did what he had to do. He had trained to be the killer we all feared from birth, but that is nae the man he is now."

"I made an oath to ye years ago, ye might nae remember, but I do," Callum said quietly. Darra thought hard to recall; she remembered asking him to run away with her but couldn't recall an oath. Finally, after a moment of silence, she shook her head. "We were young then, and I was in love with ye. Ye didnae notice because ye fancied some guard of the keep with flowing blonde hair and couldnae be bothered with me."

Darra looked down at her tied hands as he spoke; the memory of the tall blonde guard crossed her mind. She and her sister Deidre would spend hours talking about how handsome he was. The blonde guard was everything they pictured their husbands to be. *Henry. How could I have forgotten him?* she recalled as Callum paused to blow upon the fire's glowing embers. She remembered feeling heartbroken when he was married. She had been only sixteen, and he hardly noticed her, but she had an intense crush on him, convinced it was true love. Henry left her family's service and started a family of his own. Callum, a close friend at the time, found her crying over it and comforted her. Darra made him promise never to leave her, and he swore he wouldn't.

"We were just kids, Callum. That wasnae a true oath," she said after a few moments in an exhausted tone.

"It was to me, and I have always intended to stay true to it. But, despite what Carrigan may have told ye about his past, I've seen him on the battlefield, and I ken who he truly is. I willnae trust yer safety as long as ye're by his side." He paused for a moment after speaking and looked Darra straight in the eyes. "I will do anything I must to ensure ye're safe."

A sickening feeling crept over her, and she decided it best to change the subject. She didn't want to think about what

Callum would do if Samuel appeared. So she sat in silence as he tended to the fire. It was a brisk night, and being improperly dressed for the elements, Darra welcomed the warmth. She wore the same thin dress she'd worn the night before with Samuel, and she couldn't stop shivering. Once the fire was roaring, Callum opened a small sack of rations and divided the contents between them. Darra had a slice of stale bread and some dried meat for supper.

"When we get to the Morrison Clan, we'll have plenty more to eat," Callum said as he saw the disappointment on Darra's face. She nodded and silently ate the food provided, not realizing until then just how hungry she was. However, eating with her hand tied proved more difficult than she would have thought.

"Could you untie my hands to eat at least? It's not as if I'll go anywhere. I have no clue where we are, and I donnae have the skills to find my way back," she asked in a dry tone. Callum slowly stood and walked towards her. He knelt before her and began untying the knots around her wrists. His hands brushed against hers, and she felt the urge to jerk her hands away but resisted it. It was hard for her to believe there was a time when she longed for him. Moments when they might sneak out and share a small kiss, he would hold her face like a dream. Now, his callused hands grazed hers, and she felt repulsed by it.

He finished untying her and lingered in front of her for a moment. Darra was uncomfortable and shifted back on the fallen log she sat on. She quickly stood up to stretch her legs, but Callum blocked her by standing right in front of her.

"I just need to stretch my legs, Callum," she calmly said as he inched closer to her. She could feel the heat of his breath on her and wanted to turn and run as far from him as she could. But, he refused to move, and she could feel the air grow heavier around her, panic spread through her, and she felt as if she couldn't breathe.

With one quick movement, he took a step forward, placed one hand on her lower back, and pulled her tight to him. She couldn't turn her head aside quickly enough to avoid his lips landing on hers. She winced as if his touch were painful and pushed his chest as hard as she could to get him off her. When he backed away, she saw a confused look on his face. She tried to back away from him slowly. However, in a panic, she backed right into the log she had been sitting on, falling backwards with a shriek.

Samuel felt his muscles begin to ache and his bones tire after a few hours of guiding his horse through the woods so that he could track on foot. He grew more worried every moment that Callum would not stop to rest until he reached his destination, or at least far enough away where it would be impossible to track. *What if I don't find them?* Up to this point, he'd been able to keep his mind focused on finding them instead of being weighed down by dark thoughts.

I won't stop until I find her, he repeated in his mind as often as he could to fuel his trek through the dark woods. He pushed his body past the aches and pains to keep going. There was no time to stop. He could rest when he was back home with his wife.

Travelling at night could be dangerous; there was a chance he might encounter a wolf or a bear. He had to stay alert to avoid hazardous situations, and he prayed Callum would do the same with Darra in his company. She'd already fallen prey to the dangers of the wood once, and he still hadn't forgiven himself for it.

Walking as quietly as possible, he thought he heard the sounds of a faint scream. He quickened his pace to follow the direction from which it came. After navigating through the woods for a few minutes, he followed the scent of smoke. He said a silent prayer to himself that it was the two of them camping, and he was close enough to rescue his wife. As he approached, he began to question himself, *what if she wanted this?* He felt a sinking in his chest at the idea of it. She was his wife, and he knew that he loved her. He wished he had told her before she left that morning, but he hadn't. What was he to do if she wanted to stay with Callum and run away? Would he take her against her will, the woman he loved resenting him for the rest of their lives? No, if he discovered this was her plan, he resigned himself to let her be happy. No matter how hurt he would be, he loved her, and her happiness now meant more to him than anything else.

The light of their campfire came into view after a few minutes, and Samuel slowly approached. Behind a fallen tree, he could make out the silhouette of a man. The man was in front of the fire, standing and looking down at the ground. He watched for a moment and saw a slight movement in front of the rotting wood. *Darra?* He thought as he strained his eyes to look closer and make out the shapes. Unfortunately, it was too dark to see anything for sure, so he watched the man closely instead. Slowly, the man stepped over the tree, leaned down to the ground, and pulled up another person. Darra? he thought, and he immediately sprung into action.

"Get off me!" It was Darra. Leaping from his hiding place, Samuel rushed towards the fire. He saw the man pull her closer to him as she pushed him away with a struggle.

"Unhand her!" he yelled, making it to the fire just in time to see Callum release Darra and swivel to face Samuel instead. He rested his hand on the hilt of his sword and glared at him. Darra rushed behind Samuel. He drew his sword without breaking eye contact with Callum. Rage boiled within Samuel; what had this bastard done to his wife? He would pay dearly. Callum smirked at Samuel and slowly drew his sword from the sheath.

"I was hoping it wouldnae come to this, but I'm prepared, nonetheless," he said calmly, as if he were not about to engage in battle with Carrigan the Cruel.

Samuel assessed him closely, slowly inching forward. Initially, he had planned to honour Laird Sloane's request that he - Laird Sloane - be the one to punish Callum. But watching Callum touch his wife against her will infuriated him beyond all he'd ever felt.

Laird Sloane's request was about to be ignored.

He lunged forward with his sword and hit the steel of Callum's blade as he blocked the blow. Callum quickly countered the move with a swing of his own, which Samuel dodged easily. The two parried each other for a short while during the fight. He was surprised Callum could keep up with him. He had trained his entire life for battle; swinging a sword was as second nature as breathing to Samuel, and most men wouldn't stand a chance against him. Perhaps Callum was simply fortunate that he didn't intend to kill him, for if he had, the fight would have ended much sooner.

The clang of steel mingled in the air with the grunts and groans of the two exhausted men as they continued fighting. Samuel realized during that time that Callum must not be half as exhausted as he was and likely had just enjoyed his evening meal by the fire. Samuel had travelled on foot and hadn't eaten since long before he discovered Darra missing. He could feel his muscles tiring and failing him with every swing and dodge, Callum had proven himself an adept fighter, and he now feared he would fall to one of his blows.

Samuel dug deep within himself to muster the strength to win. He thought about Darra and how afraid she must have been just before Samuel arrived, taken from her home against her will for the second time and the pain that must have caused her. He gripped his sword in both hands and raised it above his head but hesitated too long as he found his strength. Then, with Samuel's chest exposed, Callum lunged and slashed him with the cold steel.

He froze for a moment and looked down at his chest. His linen shirt had been cut open, and he could see the significant slash now dripping with blood across his chest. Darra yelled something behind him, but all he heard was the muffle of her voice. He inhaled and felt a sharp pain as he tried to breathe. He groaned and stumbled for a moment, his eyes locked on Callum, who had a smirk on his face. Darra appeared at Samuel's side with her hands raised in surrender. Samuel shook his head and tried to tell her to move back, but no words made it past his lips. Darra, acting on instinct and adrenaline, dropped to her knees, crying and begging Callum to put down his sword.

Samuel steadied himself for a moment while Callum was distracted with Darra, and he prepared to lunge. Then, incredibly, he raised his sword again and, with a blood-curdling scream, charged Callum, knocking him prone on the ground, his sword falling from his hands. Samuel dropped his sword and began hitting Callum with his bare fists. He attacked him ruthlessly - as if possessed - for a moment as Darra screamed for him to stop.

~

Darra was shaking as she tried to bind Callum's hands with the same rope he'd used to tie hers. Unfortunately, she wasn't well-practiced at tying knots.

Aside from lacing on dresses and corsets, she had no need. She was sure Samuel would be much better suited to it; however, he was recovering from the battle. She moved meticulously, tying them tight to ensure it would be difficult to break free. She replayed the fight in her mind's eye as she did so, unable to stop the tears from flowing down her cheeks.

She had hoped and prayed Samuel would find her, and if he did, she knew Callum intended to put up a fight. But seeing Samuel in a duel with him had frightened her. She'd spent weeks with him and finally shared his bed. She thought she knew him and could look past his history with war and combat, but now that she had firsthand experience, it would be hard.

She had to pull him off Callum so he wouldn't kill him with his bare hands, and she had no doubt he would have if she hadn't stopped him. The look in his eyes had terrified her. They didn't resemble the eyes she stared into as they had dinner on his balcony. They were no longer gentle and calm but instead *feral*. He looked like he could not control himself, similar to the wolf that had attacked and injured her. She did not like that side of him at all.

Once Callum was securely bound, Darra walked to Samuel, groaning in pain from the wound on his chest. He had taken his shirt off and used it to apply pressure to his injury to stop the bleeding. The cream-coloured linen was red from all the blood. She walked over to him and took it so he could relax as she tended the wound. She applied pressure for a few minutes in silence, careful not to meet his eyes, afraid of what she might see.

"Are ye alright," Samuel asked after a moment. She nodded and looked down at her hands, now soaked in blood. The wound wasn't deep enough to be fatal, but it would need medical attention soon, or he might risk infection. "I was so worried he hurt ye."

She finally looked at his face and saw the Samuel she had come to know and love over the past few weeks. She was still frightened by what she saw but was no longer afraid of him. She looked into his eyes, heavy with exhaustion, and realized how spent he must be.

"We need to get ye back home soon," she said softly. She looked around the camp for Callum's belongings and found a change of clothes folded inside. She helped Samuel to his feet and tied a gray tunic around his chest as a makeshift bandage. She could see small traces of blood seeping through the fabric almost immediately.

With Samuel's weakened help, the pair lifted Callum onto his horse. Painfully, Samuel mounted his steed and led the way back to the keep, with Darra behind.

They made it to the keep grounds in the early morning hours. Callum had woken from his unconscious state shortly before they arrived, but Darra had gagged him so he wouldn't speak, although he continued to mumble and make noise. As they made it through the garden, one of the keep workers rushed to assist. Calls went out to locate Janice, the healer.

Upon reaching the keep entrance, one of the grooms ran over, helped them down from their horses, and grabbed the reins to lead them off. Even the horses looked exhausted. They, like Samuel, hadn't eaten or slept in over a day. *But, at least they hadn't sustained any injuries*, Samuel thought as he looked down at his chest covered in a blood-soaked tunic.

Several people now streamed out through the front doors of the keep toward them. Darra's sister, Deidre, ran to her and embraced her tightly. Deidre was closely followed by the twin chambermaids Kailee and Keiren, who were gushing over how worried they'd been for Darra. Angus walked through the door with Laird Sloane, who also breathed a sigh of relief to see his daughter unharmed and returned to her new home. Then, everyone's eyes fell upon Samuel and the bloody wound on his chest.

Samuel had a legendary reputation in combat. He was known for remaining uninjured, untouchable even. It was not unheard of for the best fighters in the land to acquire a nasty scar or take a more substantial injury in battle, but Samuel was as quick as he was strong and catching him with a blade was unheard of until now. Looking in the crowd at the stunned faces, he couldn't help but feel part of his self-esteem slipping away.

Laird Sloane directed a few of his guards to Callum, and they dragged him off towards their temporary quarters - tents erected in the garden. Angus walked down the steps quickly and wrapped an arm around Samuel's waist to help him inside. They moved quickly through the halls toward his chambers, Darra following close behind. Angus was anxious to learn what had happened, but Samuel could hardly think from his exhaustion, let alone speak.

"Samuel and Callum battled, and Samuel took a blow to his chest," Darra said as she closely followed behind them.

They made it to Samuel's chambers, where Janice, the healer, had unpacked her bag. She laid bandages, ointments, tonics, and several other strange tools on a table beside his bed. Angus slowly helped him lay down while Janice prepared everything. Darra moved to the opposite side of his bed and knelt, placing a hand on his arm. He looked at her and tried to muster a half smile but struggled. He could see the worry on her face.

The wound on his chest had been aching for hours. The bleeding had never had a chance to stop due to the constant movement while on horseback. He was afraid of what Janice would see when she cut through the linen covering the gash. In addition, he felt he might have broken or fractured ribs because of how painful breathing was. Janice approached him with scissors in her hand and gently began cutting the linen off his torso. When she finished, she slowly peeled back the makeshift bandage. Samuel winced as the clotted blood on the fabric clung to the wound, and she had to use more force to remove it. He knew it was bad before looking for himself. Darra inhaled sharply and quickly looked away from his chest while giving his arm a tight squeeze.

He looked down and saw a large bruise behind the wound, and off to his right side, there was another one forming. The injury itself wasn't as bad as he thought it would be. Before he saw it, he imagined it would be discoloured and jagged, but it was a bright red and a relatively clean cut. It would need to be sutured, but it wasn't deep enough to cause much damage unless it became infected - in which case, it could turn fatal. The bruising on his body was unexpected, though. He looked at Darra and squeezed her hand tightly as she watched.

"Do ye think it'll leave a scar?" he feebly asked Janice with a slight hint of a smile. He laughed to himself for a moment, then winced at the pain. Janice didn't answer him. Instead, she gave him a terse look to indicate she didn't appreciate his joking about something too serious.

"Ye might want to step out of the room, my Lady. The suturing will be very unpleasant to watch," Janice said to Darra. Darra looked at Samuel, and he nodded to assure her he'd be alright in the care of Janice.

"I'm in bonnie hands," he said to her, squeezing her hand with his before she left.

Janice quickly began to work on the wound. She poured some sort of fluid onto a cloth, dabbing it all over the surface of the cut. It caught Samuel off-guard, and he winced and groaned as his chest seemed to burn. It must be alcohol. He looked at the bloodied cloth as she put it down before grabbing another cloth and repeating the process again. Each time she dabbed, she applied more and more pressure. After she was finished cleaning the wound, Janice began threading a small string through a needle she would use to suture him. He made sure not to look at his abdomen as she began tugging his flesh back together, and he was thankful the solution she used numbed his skin. Even so, slight yelps and groans escaped his lips as he lay under Janice's care.

~

Darra waited outside his chambers while Janice tended to Samuel's wounds. She could hear his pained groans and sighs as Janice and her assistants treated him, tearing her apart inside. *This whole situation is my fault,* she thought to herself. She felt so guilty for putting Samuel in this position. *Samuel would be fine if I'd just left the room when I discovered Callum was there and called for someone to remove him.* Part of her knew she was a victim here, being drugged and stolen away from her home, but she couldn't help feeling responsible.

After a few minutes of waiting outside of her chambers, Deidre came and gave her a comforting hug.

"Are ye alright?" she asked her in a concerned voice.

"I'll be fine, just a bit shaken up, is all," Darra replied with a nod. She was thankful she had not been hurt by Callum but felt violated. Callum had kissed her twice now when she had not wanted him to and had nearly forced her into marriage with him. She felt like she had lost all control over her own life and was overwhelmed with anxiety.

"There's no rush for it, but father wants to speak with ye about what happened. He plans to properly punish Callum for all he's done to you," Deidre replied softly. Darra nodded in response. Deidre stayed with her until Angus emerged from Samuel's chambers with an update on Samuel's condition.

"He'll be fine, there might be a slow recovery for his ribs, but he'll still live a long, happy life," Angus said to her with a smile. "Now, ye need to rest. It's been a tumultuous journey for all and waiting at his bedside willnae help him heal any faster."

"Thank ye, Angus, but I wouldnae find myself anywhere else while he's in this condition," she replied calmly.

"I understand, Janice just finished, and she's brewing him a strong tea to sleep now." Angus bowed his head and walked down the hall away from her.

Darra gently pushed the door open and walked back into the room. Samuel laid still in his bed, though now a fresh bandage wrapped around his chest, and he breathed heavily from the pain. Janice dabbed a bit of sweat from his brow before pouring him some tea. Darra quickly walked to his side and sat down next to him. She held his hand and squeezed it.

"I'll be here for ye if ye need anything, anything at all," she said to him in a low voice. Janice held the cup to his mouth, and he purposefully drank the tea. Janice packed her tools and left the room. Darra could plainly see Samuel was exhausted, and the tea quickly took its effect upon him. *I wonder if that's what Callum used on me,* she thought, fighting back the stinging in her eyes. She knew crying over it would serve no purpose.

"I'm sorry I wasnae there sooner," Samuel mumbled to her as he tried to force himself through the fog in his mind and stay awake.

"Samuel, ye were there just in time. I cannae possibly thank ye enough. All that matters now is that we're both home, alive and together," she replied earnestly. She lifted his hand to her mouth and kissed the back of it before resting it on her lap. "Get some rest, I'll be right here, and I'm nae going to leave yer side."

Samuel woke as the sun rose with a painful grunt as he tried to sit up. His chest was sore, and moving his muscles proved difficult. Darra woke when she heard him and moved to help him.

"How are ye feeling?" she asked anxiously as she helped him stand up. He nodded towards the balcony, and she helped guide him over.

"I feel like I've fallen from a mighty cliff," he said with a soft sigh. "But I could be much worse than I am."

"I'm so sorry this happened to ye," Darra quickly replied. " I feel like this is all my fault. I should have done something to prevent all of this from happening. I-"

"Ye've done nae wrong," Samuel interrupted sternly. "This is all Callum's doing, do nae blame yerself. I would have searched day and night until I found ye and died fighting should it have come to that." It was true; he would not willingly have let Callum take her away from him. He watched Darra's face as he spoke, her eyes fell to the ground, and he sensed the shame she was feeling.

"Before everything happened, I found him in my chambers," she paused for a moment and fiddled with her hands. Samuel could tell she was nervous, and it worried him. "When I left yer bed that morning, he was waiting for me. He had been there all night. Before leaving home to become yer bride, I was scared. I had heard many stories of your cruelty in battle, and I desperately didnae want to come here. So, I begged him to help me, and that's what he thought he was doing."

"But ye tried to stop him?" Samuel asked her with a confused look.

"Of course. There was nae talking to him, though. He was convinced I was in danger here. He was delusional," she said pointedly. "I tried to tell him I was fine, and I sat him down to explain everything; that I didnae need him anymore-"

"Anymore?" Samuel interrupted her. He grew more confused with every word. He was starting to worry that there was more to Darra and Callum's relationship than Laird Sloane had led him to believe, that perhaps something more secretive had transpired.

"Aye. Before ye ever proposed the treaty with my father, Callum and I thought we'd marry," Darra said with a sigh. She looked at Samuel apologetically. He was taken aback by the news, feeling like he'd just been hit in the gut. "It was just talking, he was an auld friend, and it seemed the right thing to do at the time. We shared a couple of kisses in secret, but nae more serious than that, Samuel."

"Why didnae ye tell me about any of this before?" Samuel asked with a sigh as he slowly sat down on one of the chairs. "Especially since he was here. In my home." He wasn't upset that she had a prior relationship, but the idea that she had kept this a secret frustrated him.

"I didnae ken how you would react. I didnae have a chance to tell ye before they arrived, and I was shocked by his presence," she said in an apologetic tone. Samuel nodded and looked at her.

"Have ye spoken with yer father about what he plans to do about him yet?" he asked.

"I'm going to speak to him today. I just wanted to be with ye last night." She paused for a moment and stared at him. "Thank you, Samuel. Ye were my one and only hope to be rescued. I ken I could rely on ye."

A few hours later, Darra and Samuel found Laird Sloane. They provided him with all the details regarding the matter with Callum so he could make an informed decision. Callum was being held and guarded in an old shed on the grounds of the keep while they awaited Sloane's judgment.

Given the information provided by Darra, Laird Sloane thought the punishment of a week at the pillory in the center of the Sloane clan's village, followed by a season of hard labour and eventual banishment from the clan, was just.

Darra was glad Callum would have to face up to the crime he committed, but a part of her had once cared for him and worried it was the promise she made him take or her comments before she left that had driven him to this. Deep down, she knew she was somewhat responsible for his actions and subsequent punishment.

After their discussion, she returned to her chambers, where Kailee and Keiren had drawn a bath for her. She hadn't had a chance to wash since her ordeal and was pleased to have the opportunity to now. She quietly cried as she recalled the fight between Samuel and Callum and how bestial Samuel had seemed. She was overwhelmed with the guilt that Callum's ex-communication would be partly on her own hands.

When she finished, the twins helped her pick out clothes for the day. Her family was due to leave the following morning, and tonight would be their farewell feast. Not only would she be saying goodbye to her father and sister, but Samuel would send his half-brother Duncan off as a ward for the Sloane clan until they could produce an heir to take it over. Darra was sad she hadn't gotten to know Duncan well, mainly because she knew Samuel had a strong bond with him.

"Orla made some special tarts for them all as a parting gift," Keiren said to Darra excitedly while she braided her long hair. "They're Duncan's favourite, so she wanted to make them for him."

"'Tis a shame the festival we planned didnae happen," Darra said quietly. "It would have been the perfect farewell party." The twins agreed and began talking about how excited they had been about the music and food they had arranged. Darra tuned them out for a moment as an idea popped into her mind. *It isn't too late at all.*

She sprang into action with the twins behind her. All the equipment was still together in the garden, they still had all the decorations, and Orla had bought all the food they needed for the clan to feast. So, there was plenty of time to bring it all together and let everyone know the festival would go ahead.

Darra enlisted the help of the grooms to run into the village and get the word out to the townsfolk; they were to arrive at dusk, bringing Matilda the baker and Daniel the musician back with them. They excitedly agreed to the task and set off to help.

Before she announced the change of plans to everyone in the keep, she realized she would first need to inform Samuel. She had been hasty in deciding to have the festival tonight without first clearing it with Samuel before acting.

She found him pouring over some documents in his study and rubbing his temples with his thumb. She instantly regretted her impulsive decision, having not considered Samuel's obvious state of exhaustion until now. Instead, she focused on giving her family a proper sendoff and rushed into it without his blessing.

"How are ye feeling?" she asked quietly as she sat across from him.

"I'm doing fine. It's just hard to focus right now," he said with a long sigh.

"I'm sorry," she said, reaching across his desk to hold his hand. He lifted her hand to his mouth and kissed her knuckles softly.

"So, I was thinking," Darra started saying slowly, "since tonight is the last night Duncan and my family will be here, it might be nice to give them a proper farewell-"

"The festival?" he said quickly, interrupting her. She nodded at him with a nervous smile. "Angus already told me it was back on.

I'm looking forward to it." Darra breathed a sigh of relief and smiled at him.

"I'm sorry I didnae ask ye first. It all happened quickly."

"It's fine. After the week we've had, I think a little merriment is well deserved for everyone." He smiled at her when they spoke, and she felt comforted by him. She nodded her head in agreement.

"What of Shannon?" She nearly forgot about her with everything going on. "It's Duncan's last night at the keep. Will she be back to say goodbye?" Samuel's gaze fell downward, and Darra knew something was wrong.

"She wouldnae allow that to happen," he replied with a long sigh, "and she cannae go along with him. We couldnae think of any other way to handle it."

"Does Duncan ken what's gonnae happen?" she asked in a low voice. She felt her heart ache for Shannon and Duncan. Darra had lost her mother at a young age and knew the pain it caused. Shannon would still be alive but living without her would hurt Duncan. She couldn't even imagine what Shannon would feel learning her son wasn't here when she returned.

"Angus told him. He's excited to see some new places and meet everyone at the Clan Sloane." Darra saw the sadness in his eyes when he spoke. She knew he loved his brother as well. This couldn't have been an easy decision for any of them.

"Deidre will take excellent care of him there," she replied with a reassuring smile.

She left his study and informed the rest of the staff at the keep of the plans. Together they quickly set into action to prepare the garden for a large festival to accommodate most of the clan. Darra did most of the decorating in the garden by herself; she hung beautiful floral wreaths and ribbons around the greenery. Orla and the twins helped construct a few long tables and cover them with plates and cutlery for all the guests.

Dusk fell quicker than Darra had anticipated, and she was still finishing up the decorations when people began to arrive. Nevertheless, she happily greeted them and welcomed them into her home. Daniel started to play pleasant melodies as the party began. The twins sat at a table with Deidre and giggled as they stole quick glances at Daniel.

Darra rushed inside to change before more people arrived on the grounds. She decided to wear the cream-coloured dress on top of a white linen chemise. On the overdress, small silk inlaid filigree flowers slightly stood out. She tied a few small flowers to her braid and made sure she looked alright before leaving.

She searched through the keep for Samuel. She thought it would be best for them to make their official entrance together. She found him in his chambers, struggling to lace up a pair of boots. She quickly rushed over to help him with it but could tell he was frustrated with himself for not being able to finish such a simple task.

"Ye did a great job decorating," he said as she finished lacing his boots. "It looks bonnie; everyone is gonnae love it." She smiled at him and stood up.

"Thank ye," she walked over to the balcony to see how many people had arrived. She saw most of the tables full, and her heart skipped a beat. She took a deep breath and walked back to Samuel. He held his arm out for her, and she held it as they left the room and walked into the garden.

When the village folk saw Samuel, several people began whispering to themselves. He might not look injured now, but he walked with a slight limp, and the pain in his chest caused him to wince now and again when he moved. Darra and Samuel found their spots at one of the tables and joined the party.

At least a dozen people introduced themselves to Darra and congratulated her on the wedding. They were all very thankful to be attending the festival as well. Some even presented her with small gifts as a token of their appreciation. A young girl introduced herself and gave Darra a bundle of flowers she knew were all picked from the wreaths she'd hung earlier in the day, but it warmed her heart to meet her anyway.

Darra watched the crowd of people laughing and talking with a full heart. Initially, she wanted to throw this party to thank the clan for trying to find her when they didn't even know her. However, when she went into the town to find people to help, she saw a devastated, lifeless place torn apart from the struggles of war. She wanted to try and breathe life into this place, and she finally saw that she could. Her new clan smiled, laughed, sang along with Daniel, and danced. She couldn't have been happier with the result of the party.

After about an hour of arriving, when people were sufficiently fed and in a good mood, Darra walked over to the small stage erected and asked Daniel to step down for a moment. The crowd looked at her and fell silent as she stood on the stage staring at them all. She could feel her heart racing as she looked at their silent faces.

"Thank ye all for coming here tonight on such short notice," she said nervously. "I'm sure by now ye're all aware of why we couldnae do this yesterday as planned. And because of that, I now have another reason to thank ye all. When I started planning this, it was to thank ye all for coming to my aid when I found myself lost in the woods. It warmed my heart to ken ye all had searched for me and tried to help even though most of ye had never met me.

"Now, ye all did the same with the events of the past few days. Except I've met a few more of ye, and many of ye've gotten to ken me better. I couldnae be happier with the people of my new clan. This is my home now, and I feel so welcomed by ye all." Her voice cracked slightly, and she took a deep breath to compose herself. Samuel stood from his chair, walked to the stage, and stood right next to her. He held one arm around her waist and smiled at her as she spoke.

"Thank ye all so much. Coming here initially was scary, but I feel it is my home now." She looked at Samuel and smiled. "I wouldnae want to be anywhere else."

She nodded to the crowd and stepped off the stage with Samuel. The people clapped, and a few walked over to her and thanked her for the party. They told her how much it meant to have something to look forward to again. She promised them it wouldn't be the last time they celebrated this.

"Can I talk to ye for a moment," Samuel whispered in her ear as they walked through the crowd. She nodded and followed him inside the keep to his chambers. He led her out to the balcony, and they sat at the small table that looked out over the party.

"So many people came," she said with a huge smile.

"Ye did a wonderful job. I'm sure the clan will come to adore ye," he paused for a moment and looked at her. "They'll adore ye as I do. Darra, I wanted to tell ye how much I care about ye. I'd do anything to make ye happy and protect ye. I'm so sorry that we've had as many difficulties as we have in this short time, but I promise I will do everything in my power to keep these things from happening again."

"Samuel, I care about ye too. All these things have been difficult, aye, and I ken ye're there for me, and I can count on ye." She reached across the table to grab his hand. "I'm so happy here with ye. All my life, I've been told what to do. I've never had any say in anything about my life, but here with ye I do. I cannae express how much that means to me."

He squeezed her hand and looked her in the eyes for a moment with a content smile.

"I love ye, Darra," he said softly. Darra froze for a moment, but a huge smile crept across her face, and she leaned across the table to kiss him. He leaned in a bit and winced in pain.

"I love ye too, Samuel." Their lips met again, both with eager smiles. Then, after a moment, Samuel pulled away and stood up. He gestured for her to follow him inside. She expected he would lead her back out to the party, but instead, he drew the curtains and embraced her again.

Samuel's hands lowered on Darra's back as they passionately kissed one another. She giggled as he touched her and lowered his mouth to kiss her neck.

"Samuel!" she said through a laugh, and he pulled his face away from her skin. "What about the party?"

"I think they'll be fine without us for a few minutes," he said back to her with a laugh. She stood on the tips of her toes to wrap her arms around him and kiss him again. He slowly untied her dress's laces, and the dress dropped to the floor. She pulled his shirt over his head. He blushed slightly when she looked at the large bandage across his chest. She gently kissed above the wound before untying his trousers and dropping them to the floor.

He walked to the bed and sat down, leaning his head against the headboard. Darra climbed into his lap and straddled him. He grabbed her waist and pulled her close before lowering his head to her breasts. She leaned back and moaned as he took turns with each one in his mouth. She smiled as she felt him stiffening against her. He pulled his mouth away from her breasts and held her face, kissing her once more. She lifted her hips and took him inside her with a soft moan. Samuel kissed her neck again as she thrust her hips back and forth. The more she thrust, the more she could feel him hungrily groaning against her as he was closer to climax.

He wrapped his hands around her waist and watched her body for a while as she moved rhythmically. Eventually, her body began spasming, and her moaning grew louder. He pulled and pushed her hips back and forth against himself, allowing her to feel all the pleasure she could. She cried out as she climaxed on top of him, sending Samuel over the edge with a loud groan. She pressed her forehead against his and looked him in the eyes as they both finished.

∼

The following morning, they helped the Sloane entourage as they prepared to leave the keep. Samuel was pleased with how everything had eventually turned out in the days since his father-in-law had first arrived. Laird Sloane seemed to respect him as an equal, and he would no longer fear retaliation from the Sloane army. He felt at peace for the first time in his life.

Samuel found Duncan in his chambers gathering some last-minute items he wanted to take along to his new home. He wanted to say goodbye to him and attempt to explain why he had to go with the Sloanes. Thankfully, the boy's spirits were high as he was excited about this new journey.

"I'll miss ye, brother," Samuel said as he walked into Duncan's chamber and sat on the edge of his bed. He wanted Duncan to have a good life. Samuel had been raised for war, and he wished more than anything that Duncan could have a proper childhood.

"I'll be sure to write to ye and mother every day," he said excitedly. "I'll tell ye about all my adventures and the new people I meet."

"Do ye ken why ye're going with them?" Samuel asked. He waited a moment for Duncan to respond. Duncan shook his head no. "Laird Sloane is very old, and he has no heir in the Sloane clan. And until Darra and I have a child of our own, there will need to be someone there to take over and ensure the clan is functioning well. So that's why ye're going. Ye'll be learning from Laird Sloane and following in his place. Then when Darra and I have a son old enough, he'll take over, and ye'll be his advisor, like Angus is to me"

Duncan looked at him for a moment in confusion, and at all the small toys and games he was packing away.

"Will I still have time to play?" he asked with genuine concern.

"Aye," Samuel replied with a laugh, and he gently tousled Duncan's hair. "When all the work is done, and ye have free time, ye can play whenever ye want. And I'm sure Deidre would be happy to join ye."

He left Duncan to finish packing his things. Not long after, Angus came to collect the boy so his journey could begin.

Samuel stood next to Darra at the entrance of their keep, where she hugged her family goodbye. She wept softly as her sister climbed atop her horse and turned to ride away. He wrapped an arm around her and squeezed her shoulder to comfort her as they rode off.

"We'll see them again, donnae worry."

EPILOGUE

*D*arra hadn't been happy on her wedding day. She was marrying a stranger, and none of her family or friends could attend. It occurred to her that it might be a pleasant idea to have a new one. A new wedding where they could exchange proper vows proclaiming their love for each other and start fresh with the promise of a new life together.

This time, it would be exactly as she always dreamt it would. She and the twins sent invitations to friends and family of the Sloane and Carrigan clans. The perfect decorations were planned, and Daniel, the musician, was hired to perform again. It needed to be perfect because she had a huge announcement to make.

When the day arrived, the garden was full of happy, smiling faces. She was glad to see her father and sister again, even though it had only been a few months since they'd left. Duncan was here, and Samuel had been delighted to see him. The only grim face was that of Shannon, who only smiled when gushing over Duncan and telling him how much she missed him.

Darra walked down the aisle, escorted by her father. The attendees were in awe of the wedding gown. She wore a white dress with floral lace inlays and a long, flowing trail behind her as she walked. She was genuinely radiant. Darra's long red hair was braided with golden flowers intricately woven throughout by her chambermaids. She held a bouquet of yellow flowers that seemed to soak up the sun and reflect upon her face.

Samuel's smile was broader than she'd ever seen as he watched her walk toward him. She knew he wished it could have been this way from the start, but everything they had been through had helped them grow stronger as a couple; neither would have traded it for anything else.

When it came time for the vows, Darra nearly lost her composure and cried with joy.

"I saw ye for the first time as ye approached the keep to marry me. If there was any fear or hesitation in ye, I didnea see it," Samuel said, reading from the written vows in his hands, "I saw a woman who was curious about these new lands and who had a sense of adventure and wonder. I saw a fearless woman, and now I ken how true that was. We've had more trouble in our first few months together than many would experience in a lifetime, but through it all, I've seen yer true self. A fearless, caring, loving woman who I am proud to now call my wife. I didnae ken if ye could ever love me, but ye do, and I consider myself the luckiest man alive. I love ye, Darra, today, tomorrow, every day. Forever."

"Samuel, my love," Darra started to say in a shaky voice. She took a deep breath and continued. "Ye are nothing like I ever thought ye would be. Ye continue to surprise me more and more every day, and I am truly thankful for our new life together. Ye are a reliable, strong, kind and loving man that I am so incredibly fortunate to call my husband. And I look forward to starting a family with ye. I love ye more than mere words can say, and I have something exciting to share with ye and everyone here ..."

She smiled at Samuel and squeezed his hands tightly. He looked at her in confusion for a moment, but then the broad smile across his face became even wider as he realized what she was implying. Darra turned to the crowd, some of whom were wiping their eyes, and took a deep breath.

"I am with child," she said with a smile as wide as her face. Samuel embraced her tightly and kissed her. The crowd cheered joyously for them both with the news. With the arrival of an heir, the Sloane and Carrigan clans would be at peace forever.

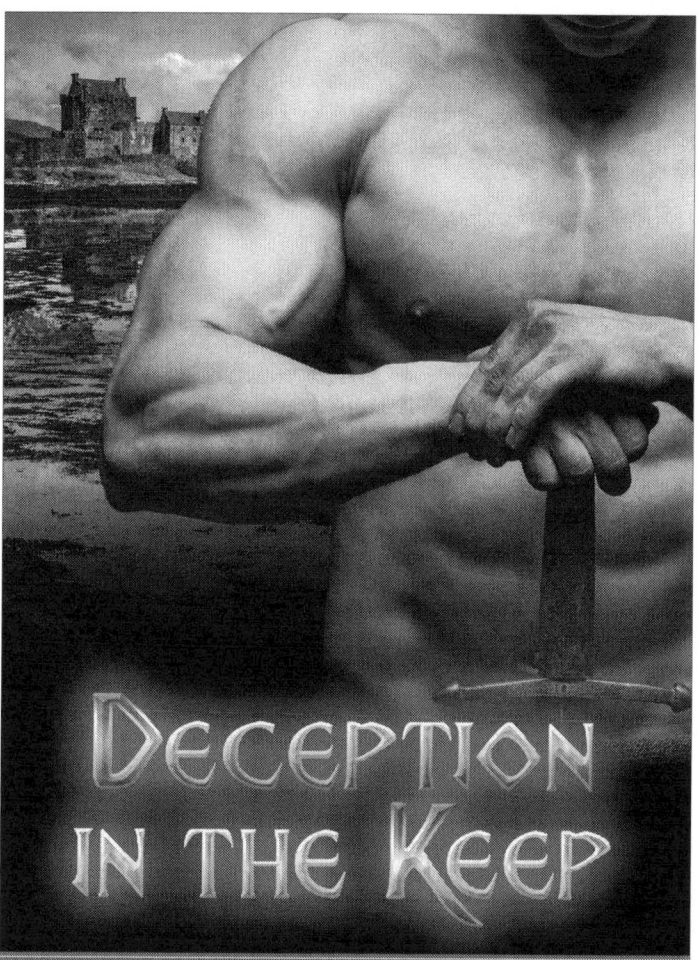

DECEPTION IN THE KEEP

Samuel had her hidden away in a small cabin in town when the Sloane clan arrived. Shannon was confused as she was swept away late in the evening by his right hand, Angus. He told her she would be fine, but she had been locked away for days. Shannon had been given plenty of food and drink, and when she asked for her embroidery tools to help pass the time, one of the men guarding her obliged and brought them to her. Regardless, she was angry, and rightfully so, she thought.

Her only hope now would be Laird Sloane taking his daughter back home.

She was furious with her stepson Samuel when she heard about the arrangement. Her late husband, Laird Ewan, would roll in his grave if he knew that his son had even thought about the treaty. He would have seen it as a coward's way out, and Shannon did too. She couldn't help but feel that Samuel had disgraced his family's name.

She confronted him about it, and all he had offered in return were lazy excuses about it being the best for the clan. *So what's best for the clan? Standing our ground is what's best for the clan. A* real *leader is what's best,* she thought.

Truth be told, she wanted her son Duncan to be their leader. Every time Samuel left for a battle, she hoped he wouldn't return. Duncan was just a boy, but she knew she could mould him into a great leader given a chance. Samuel had been raised to be a fighter; he knew the importance of being strong and cunning - yet he decided to give in to the Sloane clan.

When the wedding day came, she tried to express to him how his father Ewan would have felt. Her hatred for Samuel had grown that day, she recalled as she whiled away her time held in the cabin.

She had walked into his study early in the morning. He sat behind his desk and poured over papers. He looked up at her when she walked in and ignored her to begin working again. She stood silent for a moment, waiting to be acknowledged by him.

"What is it, Shannon?" he finally asked in an exhausted tone.

"Please rethink this. Your father would never have wanted this-"

"With all due respect," he interrupted, setting the papers down and meeting her gaze. "You hardly knew my father."

She stared at him in silence, and her eyes radiated the anger and frustration she felt towards him. How could he say that? Ewan was her husband, and she had his child. She knew him better than Samuel thought.

"I know he wouldn't have backed down to our enemies like this. All the blood spilled by our clan will be for nothing if you go through with this," she said in a raised voice. She crossed her arms and looked at him, waiting for a response.

He rubbed his temples and sighed when she spoke. "I'm no fool, Shannon. I've given every avenue thought, and this is what I've decided. If you don't like it, you're welcome to leave."

She shook her head and walked out of the room. She wouldn't stand for his disrespect much longer.

∼

Because she was family, she had to be next to Samuel during his wedding. She knew she couldn't express her disdain for their union, but she wouldn't pretend to be happy. She stood behind him at the altar with Duncan by her side. Very few were in attendance, a testament to how rushed the situation was.

The girl walked down the aisle, and Shannon felt for her for a brief moment. She was young, and there was fear in her eyes. The girl was beautiful in her wedding dress, but there was worry on her face. No doubt Samuel's reputation in battle had been her concern before she had arrived to be his wife.

Shannon's motherly instincts wanted to reach out and comfort her, to tell her she would be fine here. She knew Samuel wasn't cruel to those around him, and he would never harm her, but she couldn't do anything to show her approval. It was hard to see her here, knowing she had no choice in the union. She was plucked away from her home and brought here to live amongst strangers.

Like everyone else, Shannon didn't attend their marriage feast right after the ceremony. Instead, she returned to her room and felt defeated as she sat on her bed. She had tried as hard as she could to end this before it began, and once they consummated the marriage, all hope would be lost. If Darra were to have an heir, the clans would be one forever. *Perhaps that isn't a bad ending, though, she* thought for a brief moment before remembering how fervently her husband fought for his lands.

She smiled when an idea hit her suddenly. Certainly, Laird Sloane would not have knowingly sent his daughter to live with the man who killed her brother in battle. She laughed when she realized it was a perfect idea: tell Darra about it, and she'll be forced to leave.

She walked through the garden and picked out an orange lily before she joined the others in the dining hall. It was a beautiful flower with vibrant petals and an intense aroma - but it had a hidden meaning. It was a bad omen, subtle disapproval of their marriage.

Shannon went back to her room after she presented Darra with the flower. She didn't partake in the feast at all, assuming her message would be apparent to Samuel, and she didn't need to say anything else. He may have thought the matter done, that she would have no other stakes in the issue. He was wrong.

She spent the next few days figuring out how best to handle the situation. She could find Darra and tell her immediately, which might be enough to make Darra flee the Carrigan clan altogether. That was the best-case scenario, although a part of her wanted to hurt Samuel with this information. Any way she did it, he'd be upset, but she wanted to maximize his pain.

Shannon watched from afar as they exchanged little notes with one another. Samuel had a slight grin when he read over Darra's letter. They were a handsome couple; Shannon couldn't deny that. But the idea of Samuel finding happiness with Darra irritated her. Why should he benefit from his poor decision to protect the clan?

She decided she needed to speak to Samuel to remind him of what he did to Darra's brother. To tell him he needed to talk to his bride about it or she would. Angus was in his office looking over papers when she went to find him. She always liked Angus, he had worked with her husband, and she'd grown fond of him during the time they'd known each other.

"Oh, hello, Angus," she said as she walked in with a surprised voice. "I was expecting Samuel to be here. I'll leave you to your work."

"What did you need, Shannon," he quickly said before she could leave the office.

Shannon stopped and smiled at him. He had always been respectful to her, and she appreciated that about him. He treated her like a human when many people in the clan didn't. She married Ewan after his first wife died, and everyone thought she was only with him for his title. No one ever believed her when she said she loved or cared for him. When he died, they all assumed she'd be happy to live in the keep forever without any of the marital ties, but they couldn't be more wrong.

Truthfully, it was isolating. The only person she felt she could trust was her son, and he was a child. People assumed the worst of her, so she hardly spoke to the people there. But Angus had always been kind. He was a level-headed man she could trust would always do the right thing.

"I just need to speak to Samuel. Could you please ask him to meet with me after breakfast tomorrow?" Angus nodded his head to her, and she left the room. She felt her cheeks blush as she walked down the halls.

*T*he following day she waited in his office for an hour before he arrived. She wasn't sure if he overslept or chose to keep her waiting as a power play against her. Either way, he was already grating her nerves.

He arrived and glared at her as soon as he entered.

"What do you want, Shannon?" he said, walking around to his desk chair.

"I was just wondering if you've had a chance to tell your bride about what happened to her brother yet?" she smiled at him, watching the anger grow on his face. She could see he realized she would be a formidable obstacle to his plan, which pleased her.

"Don't you dare say anything-"

"Why, I'm offended you'd think I would! I would hate for her to find out from one of the servants."

"What is it you *really* want? Certainly, you wouldn't be threatening me without some selfish motive," Samuel said with a deep sigh.

"What I wanted was stolen from me when she arrived at the clan, and I don't think you'll be able to fix it anymore." She rose from her chair and exited the room.

∽

*S*hannon spent a lot of time in the garden when the weather was nice. It was beautifully manicured, and she enjoyed relaxing with her embroidery tools and basking in the sunlight. Days were spent walking with Duncan and playing games outside as she told him stories about how strong their clan once was. She wanted to ensure he knew they used to be fearless and would never shy away from a fight before this.

Duncan was a kind and gentle boy. He hadn't been raised to fight as Samuel had. Sometimes Shannon wished he had been so he might know the harsh history of their lands. Such knowledge would help him should Duncan ever become a leader himself. As much as she dreamt of him being a Laird someday, she feared he might be weak if it came to fruition.

Shannon was walking in the garden after supper with Duncan when she saw Samuel and Darra outside his chambers. They hadn't been in the dining hall that evening, leaving her and Angus to dine alone. Part of her enjoyed her brief reprieve with Angus to speak to him alone, while another part was eager to learn if he was telling her about his secret.

She kept one eye on Duncan and another on the new couple as they laughed and smiled at one another over dinner. She watched as they embraced on the balcony, and Samuel held Darra's face to kiss her.

"Let's go, Duncan," she yelled, storming off towards the entrance. He trailed behind her as they walked across the fresh grass into the keep. She led him to his room and told him to go to bed early before slamming his door closed and rushing down the hall to Darra's chambers.

She leaned her ear against the door and listened carefully for a moment. She heard footsteps gently make their way across the stone floor. She'd have let herself in and waited for her if Darra hadn't been there. Thankfully she wouldn't have to do that, though. She knocked on the door and paused for it to open.

As soon as it did, Shannon rushed inside, practically shoving past Darra as she did. Darra stared at her, confused as she walked into the room. It was unusual for Shannon to interact with her, much less meet her in her chamber this late in the evening. Shannon looked around the room for a moment before speaking. It was a nice room, better than her own. It was hard for her not to be envious of the fine bedding and furniture in the room when Darra had only been here for a matter of days. Shannon had lived there for years and was married to the last Laird, and her room wasn't nearly as fine.

"Listen close, child, you're married to a monster," she said grimly. She watched as Darra's mouth hung open with confusion as she searched for words and could find none with which to reply. "You think he earned the title "Carrigan the Cruel" for no reason? He's a killer. *Raised from birth* to be a killer, and I wouldn't put it past him to have some malevolent goal to which you're unaware. Don't believe me? Just ask your brother."

"What do you mean?" Darra asked in response, with a quiver of worry in her voice. A smile crept up on Shannon's face as she looked Darra square in the eyes.

"Wait, you can't, can you? He's dead, and your husband killed him." She watched Darra take in the information and shake her head in disbelief. The world crumbled before her, and Shannon felt sorry for her. For a brief moment, she regretted hurting this girl; she seemed friendly and caring. But Darra did not belong here. Shannon needed to ensure she would be leaving.

After a moment, footsteps came from down the hall and a slight knock on the door.

"Why, here he comes now. How about you ask him yourself," Shannon said with a smirk.

Samuel rushed into the room out of breath. He glared at Shannon momentarily, then quickly looked at Darra.

"Shannon, what are you doing here? We've been looking for you," he said after a moment.

"I think the two of you have something to talk about," she quickly replied before leaving the room. Shannon listened eagerly as Darra confronted Samuel, and he tried to justify his actions. A smile crept across her face as she walked away from the room.

Shannon hadn't expected Darra to run off into the woods as she did, feeling overwhelming guilt when hearing the shocking news that a wolf had attacked her. How could Shannon have possibly anticipated that reaction? She had to find a way to fix this.

It was likely that Darra would still be quite angry with Samuel, as she rightfully should be. But how would she react when she was better? Shannon hadn't seen her since she returned, but she'd heard stories of how battered she was with a considerable arm injury and a head wound.

She spent some time in her room alone, thinking of how to proceed.

Samuel had refused to leave his new wife's side since she'd been back in the keep. So Shannon snuck into his office since he wouldn't be there to stop her. She knew they had been exchanging letters with one another, which gave her an idea.

She rifled through the drawers in his desk to find one of the letters. After a few minutes of searching, she found one of the folded letters and quickly tucked it into her skirt. She would copy Darra's handwriting and send a letter to Darra's father, Laird Sloane. Should, for any reason, he believe his daughter unsafe here, Sloane could bring an end to the wedding contract himself. That would leave Samuel alone, and the war would resume.

She hoped that was the case anyway. The sooner Samuel was back fighting against the Sloanes, the better for her.

As she was leaving his office, Angus approached her. He was walking down the hall towards it - he often tended to some of Samuel's duties there, and now he likely had even more to look over with him indisposed.

"Shannon, good morning," he said in a cheerful voice. A soft smile rose on his face, and his blue eyes shone against the candles burning in their sconces.

"Hello, Angus," she paused momentarily to think of an excuse for her presence there. "I was looking for Samuel to ask about poor Darra's condition. Have you seen him?"

"Oh, he's with her now. He feels quite responsible about the whole situation. Darra will be fine, though. Janice has patched her up, and she'll recover with time." He looked at her for a moment as she nodded her head. "Would you care to join me for lunch? I was going to grab some documents to look over as I ate, but I'd be honoured to have your company instead."

"I would like that very much," Shannon responded with a smile. The more time she spent with Angus, the more comfortable she felt around him. He was an older gentleman, but he was still handsome. His dark brown hair was peppered with gray, as was his beard, and his voice had a raspy gruff that many men developed with age. His demeanour was calm and kind, no matter the situation, and she liked that about him.

He extended his elbow for her to grab hold of, and she happily took it. She blushed when she felt the heat of his body next to hers and felt her gait lighten as they walked into the dining hall. He sat across from her as they were served a thin broth with fresh bread with a flaky pastry to enjoy afterwards.

There were several moments of silence between them, Shannon could tell he was withholding information regarding Samuel and Darra, and she was trying not to ask more. She knew any loyalty he had would be towards Samuel, and if he sensed her plans, he might spoil them before she could act.

But the more she thought about it, the more she realized he might be willing to help her. Angus was her husband's closest ally. He was a counsellor and a friend to him all his life. So it might be him if anyone cared about his legacy and keeping the clan strong as he wished. But broaching the subject could prove to be risky. She would need to make him suggest it.

"How have you been lately," Angus asked as he finished his soup. "I know things have been...awkward since Ewan passed."

She wasn't sure how to answer the question. Shannon wasn't one to share her feelings openly with anyone, but she liked Angus and didn't want to brush him off.

"It has been strange," she said hesitantly after a moment. "Sometimes, I'll walk into the dining hall and expect to see him at the head of the table or in his office behind his desk. But he isn't there."

"I feel the same way," he replied with a soft smile. "He and I practically grew up together. He was like a brother to me. Walking into his office and not seeing him there is always jarring."

"For what it's worth, Ewan spoke very fondly of you. He cherished your friendship." She reached across the table and squeezed his hand. Meeting his eyes for a moment, her heart skipped a beat. Angus placed his other hand atop hers and softly squeezed it. They held them together before Shannon removed her hand and broke their eye contact.

"Thank you," Angus said as he looked down at his food and cleared his throat. "It was nice to chat with you. I hope we can do this again soon."

Shannon nodded her head silently and stood from her seat.

"I would love to have dinner sometime. I need to check on Duncan for now, though. If you'll excuse me." Angus nodded his head, and she walked out of the dining hall.

She went to her room and sat on her bed for a moment to gather her thoughts. She had her doubts about everything she was doing. Was it worth it to continue this fight if her actions had gotten Darra injured? What would Angus think of her when he learned she had been the one to spoil the peace between the clans? She was sure she was developing feelings for him and wanted to protect that. But she felt she owed it to her late husband to see his vision for his clan through, and she knew in her heart that Duncan would be a much better leader than Samuel

could ever be.

Shannon practiced writing in Dara's handwriting before beginning her forgery attempt. The letter needed to be believable, so there would be few questions from Laird Sloane. She hoped to convince him that Darra was in danger, that Darra might be harmed should she live here much longer. Then, if he came to check on her, Sloan would find his daughter wounded and would question his decision to agree to this marriage in the first place.

When she finished her letter, Shannon sealed it and brought it to one of the grooms. He happily accepted the job when offered a handsome fee for the work, agreeing to deliver it to Laird Sloane directly.

The next few days passed without any significant events. Shannon waited patiently to hear about any response from Laird Sloane and spent her time with Duncan while waiting. Since Ewan's death, she has tried to be with Duncan as much as possible. He was understandably upset when told his father had died, and Shannon wanted to ensure he was alright. But sometimes, she worried his time with her was making him too soft.

She wanted him to have fighting lessons, but Samuel refused to allow it. She was angry with him for telling her how she should raise her child. He was Duncan's brother, yes, but she should be the one to determine what he could and could not do. Samuel was adamant that since the war was over, he did not need to learn to fight and could enjoy his childhood without learning to kill.

"It's important he at least learn the basics for if he needs to defend himself," she would always argue. Samuel would respond by using his childhood as an example, having been taken from him because of the war.

Part of her understood his position and believed it thoughtful of him to want to spare Duncan. But it was necessary as a leader to be prepared for anything. Even though the war with the Sloane clan was now over, they couldn't anticipate the future. And if that meant her son needed to fight, he would need to be prepared.

She finally learned that word from Laird Sloane came a few days after she sent the letter. She was sitting outside with Duncan savouring the sunlight with a book in her hand. Duncan dug in the dirt, looking for worms and bugs to observe and poke. Samuel walked up to her with an unsealed envelope in his hand. He asked young Duncan to leave them so they could talk, and the boy jumped up from the dirt and ran inside.

"Is that for me? I've been expecting a letter for a few days now," she said calmly.

"How could you do this?" His voice was hushed, but she could sense the anger in his body language. She was afraid of him for a brief moment as he towered over her with clenched fists.

"Perhaps she isn't safe here. She is married to the man who killed her brother. Do you think Guthrie is aware you killed his heir?"

"What do you want?" he asked impatiently through his gritted teeth.

She paused for a moment and stared at him. "I *wanted* to be the lady of the clan, and I was. Then that was taken from me by some wretch from the enemy clan. I will not just let her take over these lands. I had to work for this-"

"You worked for nothing! I trained and fought for these lands. My father did the same as his father before him. All you did was seduce a widower. You have no claim to these lands, and you never will," he yelled at her and stared down with a frightening glare.

She closed her book and met his gaze. She felt a fire within her body like nothing she'd felt before. This wasn't the first time he disrespected her, and she was tired of it. She wouldn't back down and cower away from him like he wanted her to. She quickly jumped to her feet and gathered her things to leave.

"You've insulted me for the last time-"

"You've threatened me for the last time, do it again, and I'll have you sent to live off in the woods by yourself," he interrupted before turning and walking away.

Shannon watched him walk away with the letter in his hand.

Angus was sitting in the parlour, which he often used as an office when Samuel was in his. Shannon didn't expect to find him there when she opened the door to enter. She greeted him with a smile and walked to a chair to sit with him.

"I see you've been kicked out of the office," she said in a friendly tone.

"Well, it's been a hectic morning, and Samuel needed some time alone," he replied flatly.

"What was in the letter?" she asked in a hushed voice.

He sighed and rested his hands in his lap before looking at her to answer. She could tell he was upset with her. Even if there was a chance he would support the motive of what she was doing, there was no doubt it was making his life more difficult.

"Laird Sloane will be coming here to check on his daughter. He'll be taking her away if he thinks she's in danger, and the war will likely resume." He paused for a moment, not breaking his gaze with her. "Which I'm sure fits into your plan well enough."

She sighed and looked down at her folded hands in her lap. She felt ashamed when he mentioned that to her. It was what she wanted, and her plan worked flawlessly thus far, but his frustration hurt her.

"Ewan would never have stood for this treaty," she said in a low voice after a moment. "He was adamant about the clan being strong and fighting." She looked up at him, staring into his eyes. "He wouldn't approve of any of this."

"I know," he responded quickly. "He would have hated this. If Samuel had suggested this when his father was alive, he would have been outraged. But he isn't here, and this is what our Laird has decided to do, and we need to support the decision to keep the clan strong. If people sense anything is wrong, who knows what can happen."

"I'm just not sure I can support a decision that directly undermines all the work my husband did." She was quiet and resolute when she spoke.

"I understand that, and I can respect that view." He paused for a moment, fidgeting with the papers in his lap. "It is worth noting that leadership can be demonstrated in various ways. Ewan wasn't a practical man; he was a fighter. Samuel has always hated that, and he wants peace."

She nodded and sat across from him silently for a moment before leaving the room. It was difficult to hear because she'd grown to hate Samuel so much, but Angus had made many points. Samuel had never seen Darra. He did not love her before she arrived, and yet he proposed for the good of the clan. Perhaps she had been blinded by her hatred and desire to preserve her husband's legacy.

The more she thought about it, she couldn't help feeling guilty. Her actions had caused an innocent girl to run away in fear and be attacked in the woods. Darra could have died thanks to her, which was never her intention. She returned to her room and lay on her bed, thinking about her actions.

She decided she would try and make things right. When Laird Sloane arrived, she would tell him she had written the letter and apologize for it. She would try her best to tell him that Samuel cared for Darra, and she'd seen that in the short time they'd been together. Darra was safe here, and she would make sure he knew that.

∽

Shannon decided to find Darra the following day to apologize to her. She hadn't intended to cause her to run away as she did. Shannon needed to repair what her actions had broken. Unfortunately, Darra was so busy planning the festival she was working on she didn't have the chance to speak to her.

She contemplated finding Samuel and speaking to him, but she couldn't imagine it would help. He had detested her since she married his father, and anything she said would likely worsen the situation.

Just two days after the letter arrived, the bells in the keep rang, signalling the Sloanes' arrival. It was late evening, and Shannon was in her nightgown when they echoed through the halls. She looked through her window and saw horses riding down the path straight towards the entrance. She quickly dressed in a simple gown and began to make her way to the gate where everyone else in the keep would likely be gathering.

Before she could make it there, Angus met her in the hall. He stopped her and gently took hold of her arm to try and lead her away.

"What are you doing?" she asked, pulling her arm away from his.

"You can't be here while the Sloane clan is with us," he said in a hushed voice.

"What do you mean? Why not?" Her voice reflected the annoyance she felt. She turned to walk towards the keep's entrance, but Angus grabbed her. This time his grip was much stronger.

"Please just come with me, Shannon," he pleaded with her. "You don't have much choice."

She tugged her arm away from him and stormed further down the hallway. Angus didn't follow her; she felt like she'd won that small battle. However, before she made it to the end of the hall, two of the keep's guards stepped into view and blocked the exit. She turned to face Angus, standing where she'd left him with his arms by his side. Shannon thought she saw a guilty look on his face, or at least hoped she did.

With the guards just steps behind her, Shannon walked back towards Angus. She followed him through the halls to an exit at the back of the keep. Two horses were saddled and ready to depart. She felt her heart drop for a moment; she wasn't sure what was happening and worried.

One of the guards hopped onto a horse and extended his hand for her to climb up with him. She looked at Angus, and he gave her a slight nod before she extended her hand to the guard.

"They're taking you into town to stay while they're here," Angus said when she was steady on the horse. "I'm sorry, Shannon, but he can't trust what you'll do. We'll bring some more of your things in the morning."

She said nothing in response before the guard leaned forward slightly for the horse to take off.

The small cabin she stayed in was nice enough. Small and furnished, it was warm once the guards lit a fire. Shannon occupied the bedroom while the two guards remained in the common room. She waited patiently for Angus to arrive in the morning with her belongings.

If they'd have given her a moment to gather her things, she could have brought a change of clothes, her embroidery kit, and perhaps a book to read while she was being held. The guards had been instructed not to engage with her, so general conversation was out of the question.

Angus finally arrived in the late morning. He carried a small bag at his side, which Shannon could only assume were some of her possessions. She blushed at the idea of Angus going through her closet and picking out clothes for her. She felt like it was an invasion of her privacy.

"Will you tell me what is going on now?" she asked when she saw him. She was angry and did not attempt to hide it.

"Samuel is worried you'll say or do something to encourage Laird Sloane to take Darra away," he said calmly.

Angus looked at the guards in the common area sitting on wooden chairs, pretending not to hear what was happening and gestured for them to leave. They nodded their heads and stepped outside without hesitation.

"For what it's worth now, I had planned to tell the truth when I met Laird Sloane," "What you said yesterday made sense. It opened my eyes to another view. I was emotional and confused, and I acted too quickly on it."

"I'll tell him that when I see him. Maybe if he knows he might understand, you can come back earlier to clear that up."

"How long do they plan to visit?" she asked nervously, hoping it wouldn't be long.

"Just a few days. We think they'll stay for the festival," Angus replied.

"What about Duncan while I'm gone? Who will look after him?" She knew he would be in good hands at the keep. The staff loved him and would happily look after him even if she weren't there.

"He'll be well taken care of, don't worry about that," Angus replied with a smile.

She sighed and smiled back at him, staring him in the eyes for a moment.

"Thank you for coming here, Angus. I was quite stressed last night, and you've put me at ease today." He nodded in reply and handed her bag over to her.

"We've got a few changes of clothes and some reading materials in here for you," he paused and blushed as she opened the bag and looked through it. "I had to pick the clothes, so hopefully, they're to your liking."

She smiled again at the thought of Angus going through her wardrobe and trying to find matching outfits to wear while she was in seclusion. It felt like an invasion of privacy, but it was also quite funny to her.

When Angus left, he sent the guards back inside with her. They walked to their chairs and sat down without saying anything to her.

A small kitchen in the cabin had been stocked with some of the essentials needed to prepare food. Rifling through the cabinets to find ingredients, Shannon began to cook breakfast. It reminded her of the years before she married Ewan. Since living at the keep, she didn't have to cook or clean anything. Everything there was done for her, and she never had to worry about it. But prior to that, she was quite capable on her own. She had been poor and spent most of her life in a cabin only slightly bigger than this one. Her father was killed in the war when she was very young, and her mother put her and her sister to work doing various odd jobs to make a living.

At the time, she and her sister always dreamt about getting out of that environment. It was a dream come true for her to marry Ewan and live such a wealthy life. But now that she has everything she needs there, she often yearns for the humble life she had before.

She convinced herself to enjoy this time away from the keep. If she could do that, it would undoubtedly make the time go by faster, and she could see her son that much sooner.

～

Four days passed without event. Shannon and the guards had begun speaking, so she didn't feel as alone there. But she was eager to be back home to see her son and looked forward to seeing Angus again.

She was pleasantly surprised when she heard a knock on the door to find Angus walking inside the cabin. He nodded to everyone in the room and greeted them. The guards gathered themselves and stepped out of the room once again. She smiled and said hello to Angus, but his face was locked in a pained expression.

"What's the matter?" she asked in a low voice. She was worried, and dozens of things ran through her head simultaneously.

He walked over to her and gestured for her to sit in one of the chairs. She hesitantly sat down across from him. Her worry only grew while she waited for him to respond. Finally, after a moment, he took a deep breath and looked her in the eyes. They were red and full of stress. She braced for bad news, not knowing what it could be.

"The Sloanes are gone, and so much has happened since you've been here," he said slowly. She could tell he was dancing around something else with his words. "Darra was kidnapped, but she was found safe-"

"Kidnapped?" she asked in a raised voice. She had obviously missed quite a lot.

"One of the men who rode in with Laird Sloane was an old friend of hers that thought they were perhaps more than that. He planned to take her to a new clan and marry her there. Thankfully Samuel found her in time, but in the fight to protect her, he was badly wounded."

"Samuel was wounded?" she asked with even more confusion. She had very conflicting feelings at that moment. She didn't like Samuel, but she had been his stepmother for ten years. A tiny part of her had grown to care about him, and hearing he had been wounded unsettled her.

"He was. The man who kidnapped Darra - Callum is his name - he's one of Laird Sloane's best men," he said in an exhausted voice.

"What happened with Laird Sloane? Has the war resumed?"

"They were able to talk that out; everything is fine with that." He paused for a long moment. Something was choking him up.

"What else?" she asked hesitantly, her heart falling to her stomach.

"Samuel and Darra have not consummated their marriage. Because of that, Laird Sloane worries about an heir due to his health. As Darra might not be expecting a bairn anytime soon, it was agreed upon that Duncan would be his ward until there is a proper heir." He spoke slowly, and his words were delicate as he broke the news.

"I'm his mother. How was anything agreed upon without me there?" she asked in a desperate confused voice.

"Samuel decided it would be best to ensure the war did not resume. Duncan liked Laird Sloane, and Darra's sister Deidre was very kind-"

"This was not Samuel's decision!" she yelled, tears streaming from her eyes.

She felt her heart break at that moment. Her decision to try to separate Samuel and Darra led to this. She was the reason her son was being taken from his home to live with strangers. How could they have made this decision without even letting her say goodbye?

Angus walked to her chair and knelt beside her. He took her hand and squeezed it tightly. Her breath was sharp as she inhaled. She couldn't control her crying anymore.

"I'm so sorry, Shannon, I tried to think of anything I could to stop this, but it was the only option they could agree on."

"I have to go to him," she said through her sobs, standing up to go pack her things and leave.

"You can't go, Shannon," Angus said in a pained voice as he grabbed her arms to stop her.

She collapsed in his arms, and he held her while she cried and tried to comfort her as much as he could.

"I didn't even get to say goodbye," she sobbed into his chest over and over.

Eventually, she pulled herself away from him and tried composing herself as much as possible.

"I'm so sorry," Angus whispered to her as he shook his head. "Go gather your things; it's time to go back."

She nodded and walked into the small bedroom she'd been staying in. She threw her clothes and the books she'd been given in the bag and left the cabin with Angus.

The guards had already left, so she rode on Angus' horse with him. She sat behind him and held onto his waist as they rode across the hills to the keep. She was furious with Samuel and heartbroken at the same time. She wasn't sure what to do when she returned and saw him there.

They arrived at the keep in the late afternoon. The garden was full of people who looked to be cleaning and taking apart the large tables for the festival. Shannon ignored them all as she walked inside the keep. She went directly to Duncan's room.

She opened the door, knowing he wouldn't be behind it, but a small part of her still hoped to see his face. She walked to his bed and sat on the mattress, grabbing one of his pillows. She clutched it to her body and looked around the room. A small laugh escaped her when she saw most of his toys were missing. He'd taken them along, no doubt. She just hoped there was someone there to play with him.

She laid back on his bed and rested there for a while; she inhaled his scent from the pillows and softly wept into them.

After a while, she pulled herself together and left his room. She took a long hot bath and tried to relax as best she could, given the circumstances. Worrying thoughts clouded her mind. It was hard for her to believe they could take away her son without consent. She was utterly heartbroken.

After the bath, Shannon immediately went to sleep without dinner. She was too upset to even think about eating.

∼

The following day she woke up still feeling as empty as she had the night before. There were still so many unanswered questions, and she planned to get them. She dressed and composed herself in her mirror before leaving her room. Samuel simply couldn't see her in this state. She needed to be strong. She needed to show him that she was resilient.

She let herself into his office early in the morning before he made his way there. She sat in one of the chairs across from his and waited for him to arrive. After about an hour, she heard footsteps approaching and stood from her chair. The door opened, and Samuel looked at her with a surprised face. He sighed and closed the door behind him.

Seeing him ignited the rage within her, and she rushed to him and slapped him across the face. He shook his head without saying a word, and she did it again. But, again, he said nothing and accepted them both as if he'd been expecting it.

"You bastard," she said with venom in her voice after a moment.

"I understand you're upset-"

"Upset? I'm not upset, Samuel. I'm livid," she said in a raised voice. "How could you do this? You send me away in the night and send my son off to live with another clan while I'm gone. What kind of monster are you?"

"We've all made sacrifices for this clan. But, we couldn't go on much longer if the war resumed; the entire treaty depended on an heir for Laird Sloane," he said calmly. "Please take a breath and sit down. Then, I'll answer any questions you have."

He walked around to his side of the desk and sat with his hands crossed. Shannon sat across from him and crossed her arms over her chest.

"Why couldn't I go with him," she said, her voice cracking as she spoke.

"You must understand that your actions have made it hard to trust you. It was a concern that you'd convince Duncan or Laird Sloane of something, and it would spark conflict." She shook her head when he spoke and scoffed at him.

She already felt this was her fault; now, he blamed her too. She didn't need anything to make her feel worse than she already did.

"Will I ever see him again?" she asked quietly, holding back tears this time.

"I'm certain you will. Duncan will come and visit, and we'll visit them when Darra is pregnant. You can write to him, and he already said he'd write to you daily."

"That's not the same," she paused for a moment and stared Samuel in the face. "My son is going to grow up in another home. I won't get to see any of it. The next time I see him, he'll be a foot taller, and his voice will be deeper. You've taken the precious moments of his life from me."

"I'm truly sorry for that, but the decision has been made, and he is there now. There isn't anything to be done about it anymore." His tone was final. There would be no more discussion. Shannon stood from her chair, paused briefly, and left the room.

She felt defeated. Her plans to maintain her husband's legacy had failed, and now she was alone at the keep with people she despised.

She thought about leaving. If they were so concerned with her ruining things for them, it would be best to just be out of their hair. She could stay in the small cabin she was just in. It was enough for one person to live a comfortable life independently. Now that Duncan wasn't at the keep for her to look after, nothing was holding her there.

Shannon returned to her room to pack her things and prepare to leave. She heard a slight knock at her door shortly after she entered her room. Upon opening the door, Darra stood with an apologetic look on her face. Shannon stepped aside to allow Darra into the room.

They hadn't spoken since Shannon had revealed Samuel's secret to Darra. What little relationship they had was strained, most certainly. However, despite that, Shannon did not hate Darra, for she hardly knew her, and from what little she did, Darra seemed quite pleasant.

"What brings you here, Darra?" Shannon asked in a sullen tone.

"I wanted to see how you were doing since returning," she said hesitantly.

"Well, I got some of the worst news of my life since returning, so not very good," she replied with a fake plastered smile.

"I know. I can't entirely agree with the decision. I can't imagine what you're feeling. But if it is of any help to you, my sister Deidre said she'd look after him, and she's very kind. So you can trust he's in good hands with her."

Darra had a sympathetic look on her face, and Shannon could tell she really cared about this. However, it only brought a small amount of comfort, knowing he might have a friend in the Sloane clan.

"Thank you for that. But I feel the best person for that job is me, and I won't be there for him now." Darra reached her hand out to squeeze Shannon's to try to comfort her. "I'm thinking of just leaving here."

"Where would you go?" Darra asked with a concerned look on her face.

"The cabin I was held in while your family was here. It was small and quiet. Just enough for me to live by myself," she paused for a moment staring at the floor. "There isn't anything here for me now."

"Have you spoken to Samuel about it?" Shannon shook her head when Darra asked the question. "I can speak to him for you if you'd like."

"That would be lovely, thank you. He and I have never really been kind to one another." Darra nodded her head and said goodbye before leaving the room.

Shannon found a few small bags and began folding her clothes inside of them. She spent the majority of the afternoon packing her belongings to leave. She was sure Samuel wouldn't protest when Darra asked him about it. On the contrary, he would love to have Shannon out of his way to assume his leadership role without her scrutiny.

She walked to the dining hall around supper time for her first meal in two days. She hadn't realized how hungry she was until noticing the sun setting while she packed. The dining hall was full when she arrived. Samuel and Darra sat at their seats while Angus and the twin chambermaids sat at opposite sides of the table. She felt everyone was staring at her when she walked through the door.

She walked to the table and sat down next to Angus without paying everyone else any mind. Shortly after she sat down, their meals were served and she quickly ate, nearly forgetting her table manners due to her hunger.

Everyone chatted as they ate their dinner, they all told stories about the festival, and she just listened. When she finished, Shannon excused herself early to avoid more sympathetic glances and uncomfortable small talk about an event she didn't attend.

She quickly made her way down the halls toward her room. It would be possible for her to leave in the morning if she could have everything finished tonight.

"Shannon, wait!" a voice called as she walked. She turned around and saw Angus walking toward her. "I heard you want to leave the keep?"

"You heard correctly. There just isn't any reason for me to stay now."

"How soon are you leaving?" he asked.

"I was hoping to go in the morning if Samuel approved of me staying in that cabin," she quickly responded.

"I hate to see you leave, but I understand why you feel you need to," he said with a reassuring smile. "But, I recall you were promising me your company at dinner, and I'd love it if you could stay just one more day for that."

Shannon smiled and shook her head at him. She couldn't help herself from laughing along with him.

"Actually, I found myself cooking at the cabin for the first time in a while, and I'm quite good. So perhaps I can make something for us both tomorrow night?"

"That sounds just as lovely," he replied with a smile. "And Samuel has approved for you to live there. I'll find someone to help you bring your things over in the morning."

They said their goodbyes, and Shannon returned to her room to finish. She didn't have much; most of her belongings were clothes and jewelry Ewan had bought for her. She contemplated taking some of the vases in her room to make the cabin less bare, but she decided a fresh start would be the best for her.

She walked down the hall to Duncan's room, packing a few things to take. If he ever visited her there, he would have them to play with; if not, she would have small mementos to remember her son's childhood. The idea of leaving his room behind was difficult, but it wasn't his room anymore.

One of the guards that originally accompanied Shannon to the cabin agreed to help her move her things there. Together they carried the few bags she had to the keep entrance, where two horses waited for them.

When she was ready to leave, Samuel and Darra stood at the door to say goodbye. Angus stood behind them but withheld from saying his goodbyes.

"The horse you'll be riding there on is yours to keep," Samuel said as he approached her. "We haven't had a good relationship, but you're still family. My father wanted me to take care of you, and I will. If there is anything you need, please reach out. Despite what I've said in the past, you're welcome here anytime."

"Thank you," Shannon replied with a soft smile. "Samuel, I am sorry about everything I've done here. My thoughts were clouded, and I thought I was protecting the clan. But I know now that they're at peace with the decision, and I am too."

"I'm sorry for everything I've done. I know I'm not a perfect leader, and I can only hope my children and Duncan can learn to be better than me," he replied.

Shannon climbed her horse and waved to Darra before riding off behind her escort.

*I*t didn't take her long to unpack her belongings. She finished by early afternoon, and that provided plenty of time to prepare for dinner with Angus. Moving about the kitchen, she found herself growing nervous. It was peculiar. She felt as if she was a young girl again.

She made a loaf of fresh bread and a hearty potato stew she knew Angus would love. He knocked on her door just as the sun began to set, and she let him inside. He sat at the small table in the common room while she finished preparing the plates to bring to them both.

"This place has so much potential, doesn't it," Shannon said as she approached with two bowls of stew. "There's plenty of space for a garden. I can grow my own vegetables and fresh flowers and herbs. It'll be wonderful."

"It does have a bit of charm to it," he replied just before taking a bite of the stew. "You were not lying when you said you were good."

"Thank you." She blushed and smiled at him for the compliment. "I know you're a fan of Orla's potato stew, so I thought you might like this."

"Don't tell her I said this, but this one might beat hers." He took another bite and smiled as he chewed.

They made small talk as they ate their dinner. Shannon had known Angus for ten years but never had the chance to get to know him on a personal level, and Ewan never spoke about him to her aside from clan-related issues. So it was nice to share a conversation with someone who seemed genuine and caring.

"I've had a wonderful time this evening, Angus. I hope you'll come back another time to keep me company. It's a shame we've known each other all these years and haven't spoken like this before," she said as their conversation lulled.

"I would love to join you again another time,"

"I do have a small confession to make, though."

"What is it?" she asked. She was nervous given everything that had happened in the last few days. She hoped it wasn't anything to do with Duncan or the Sloane clan.

"I've had feelings for you for some time now." His face reddened as he spoke. "Since before Ewan passed, I've thought you were beautiful and strong and seeing you with Duncan, you are caring and passionate. I think very highly of you."

She couldn't help but smile at him, but she was taken aback by the confession. She felt very similar and had no idea he did too. But it felt strange because of her husband. Angus was his closest advisor and best friend. Now he worked for her stepson. If anything came of their relationship, it could jeopardize his position in the clan.

"Angus, I'm surprised to hear this. I feel the same way." She smiled and reached her hands across the table for his. "I think you're fantastic, and I would love to pursue something. But I'd be concerned about your job and relationship with Samuel. Aren't you?"

"I hadn't given that much thought, honestly," he replied. "I don't think it would matter that much."

Shannon hated that she hadn't thought of it sooner, but she was a widow. People in town would look down on her for being with another man - especially since her husband was a Laird. They might think it is disrespectful.

"What will the clan think of me for being with someone who isn't Ewan, though," she replied in a soft voice.

He shook his head and realized it too. It would be impossible for them to be together. He lifted her hand to his mouth and delicately kissed her fingers. Her heart skipped a beat when she felt his lips against her skin, and she smiled wide at him.

Angus leaned across the table and gently lifted Shannon's chin with his hand.

"Perhaps the clan doesn't need to know," he said before leaning in to kiss her.

She happily kissed him back. Her entire body felt light as if she might float away any second when he kissed her. When he pulled his face away from hers, neither could control the smiles growing on them.

Angus stayed with her a short while before deciding he best leave to avoid suspicion. But Shannon couldn't deny that the idea of a secret romance was exciting. She felt young and invigorated again at the thought.

She kissed Angus on the cheek before she watched him ride away on his horse. She felt content and excited about a new chapter in her life.

NOTE FROM FIONA

Thank you so much for reading this book.
I truly hope you enjoyed it!

If you could leave a review on Amazon, that would be so helpful!

I love reading your reviews, and they are very important to me. They help me understand what you enjoy and what I should change.

Link to leave review:
https://geni.us/LIV-complete-review

A FREE GIFT FOR YOU

Thank you for purchasing this book!
Your support means a lot to me, so I'd like to say thank you with this free gift…

VISIT HERE to claim your FREE GIFT:
https://geni.us/seducing-seamstress

ALSO BY FIONA KNIGHTLEY

https://geni.us/fiona-knightley

~

Fiona would love to hear from you!
www.knightleyromance.com

Made in the USA
Middletown, DE
23 December 2024